I REGRET NOTHING

JB TREPAGNIER

I REGRET NOTHING

I've been naughty, and I don't care.

They called it heinous. I called it a fun Friday night. That artifact was just begging to be stolen. Come on, an amulet that brings back the dead, and they just leave it on display in a museum? That had my name all over it. But now they know I'm the Silver Fox and can tie me to other thefts. They intend to put me away for a long time.

But I've made friends in Silverhold Detention Center for the Magically Delinquent. Two men who are like me. I think even the psycho prison guard might help me.

I regret nothing, and neither do they. Breaking out of Silverhold is going to be my best heist ever.

FOREWORD

This series is going to lead to FF in the harem, eventually. If you're only into the bisexual lovin' when it comes to the guys or not at all, that is totally fine, but there's FF action in this book.

REI

J threw my keys on the counter and collapsed on the couch. I spent all day scouting security in the museum. I had it down pat. I could make my move any day now. This just went against every single ounce of training from my mentor—don't steal anything you intend to keep. Don't leave evidence lying around your house. Only steal for paying clients.

This had served me well so far. I didn't even shoplift my clothing and food anymore. I paid for it with the money I earned stealing for other people. And I was fucking good at it. They even gave me a nickname on all the most-wanted lists I was on. I was called the Silver Fox by everyone who wanted to arrest me, but they didn't have a single shred of evidence to connect me to anything except a stray fox hair I left behind by mistake.

That was against my training, but I was a little proud of that nickname and that little tidbit I left behind. It didn't pull from the root, so they couldn't DNA test it. All they could tell was that it came from a silver fox. The human police thought I had a pet fox, and the magical police thought I was a fox shifter.

Honestly, I didn't know what the fuck I was, but I knew I wasn't a shifter. My mentor was a wolf shifter who took me in when I tried to pick his pocket. Hauser could have snapped my neck for trying to steal his wallet, but he liked my spunk trying to steal from a master thief in the first place. I had no way of knowing that when I tried to take his wallet. I just saw a lot of cash in there when he was paying for coffee.

I didn't need the cash. I was in college with a job and could pay for my rent and food. There was just something *exciting* about getting in trouble. I couldn't act out in college, or I'd get expelled and lose my job. But stealing totally filled that hole, and the more I did it, the more I wanted to do it.

Until I tried to steal Hauser's wallet, I never even fathomed it blowing up in my face. Hauser knocked me out and threw me into a van. I woke up tied to a chair in some remote cabin. I still remembered it. I woke up to an enormous man sitting in front of me, just studying me.

"Your technique is sloppy," he said.

I was utterly shocked. Everything I had done to lead me to that point was flashing in front of my face. He kidnapped and could have easily killed me, but he brought up my technique instead? I was in danger, but I was still me. I tried to shrug with my hands tied behind my back.

"You're the first to have caught me."

He just leaned back in his chair.

"I won't be the last either if you keep doing it like that. Stealing wallets is just so basic, and I can tell from your scent you aren't even remotely basic," he said, his eyes flashing amber.

I realized the deep shit I was in. I tried to keep my stealing limited to humans, so I didn't piss off the supernatural community. At the time, I thought I was just a fox shifter, and there were plenty in that community who would see me as prey. The first time I fucked up, it *had* to be a wolf shifter who had no problem hunting foxes.

"Are you going to kill me?" I squeaked.

The wolf just studied me.

"Why would I do that?"

"Because of what I am and what you are?"

The wolf leaned forward on his elbows and studied me.

"And what do you think you are?"

"Just a fox shifter. Please, if you let me go, I'll never steal from you again."

The wolf let out this little growl.

"Sweetie, you don't smell like any fox shifter I've ever met. You smell more like this demon I met once. But we can work with this. Hell keeps to themselves, and not many people have met a demon. If anyone asks, you're just a fox shifter. How would you like a job?"

I glared at him. I thought he was lying to me. I was just a fox shifter.

"I have a job."

"Then why did you try to steal my wallet, girl?"

I shut right up because I didn't have a logical explanation for stealing from him. I just wanted to. I saw his money, and I liked the thrill of seeing if I could get away with taking it. The wolf saw right through me.

"You didn't need my money. You just like it. I can

offer you a job that pays way more money than you're making now and will ever make in your entire life. And it's much bigger mischief than picking pockets. This is theft on a much bigger scale. The stakes are higher if you get caught."

I should have said no. I should have learned my lesson about stealing and gone back to my classes. But honestly? That sounded a lot more fun than my computer science degree and having to spend eight hours a day behind a desk utterly bored.

"I'm interested," I said.

And that was how I became a master thief. I apprenticed under Hauser and learned from the best. I stole from museums, banks, rich people. Whoever could afford my services. And I did it through a website where people mostly posted handmade goods. My shop pretended to sell bath items, but each listing meant something. Most of the soaps were bank heists. The bath bombs meant museums. The bath melts were when you wanted me to steal from someone personally. There was a listing for a custom item where anything went.

I loved every single thing about it. Hauser was more like a father to me than my adoptive father had been. He told me more about who and what I was. I was raised in America, but my adoptive parents refused to tell me from which country I had adopted. I knew I had to be Asian, even if my hair was pure white, and my eyes were violet, but they wouldn't tell me where my ancestors came from. If I asked, they would just tell me I was American and to drop it. They wouldn't talk about my birth parents at all.

They were human, and I had to keep it this big secret from them that I could either turn into a full fox or sprout ears and a tail and become way more agile. I guess we were all keeping secrets. Hauser didn't do that to me. I believed him now when he told me I smelled like a demon, and we were trying to find out what kind. The closest we could figure, I was a Kitsune, but I didn't know how I ended up topside being raised by humans.

That was still a heavily guarded secret. Both of us advertised my services as a fox shifter. Most of the supernatural community who would have looked down on me as prey were now lining up for my services. I apprenticed with Hauser for ten years, and I'd been on my own for five. I still talked with Hauser every day, and he was up my ass about this heist I planned. He should be calling soon to talk me out of it.

There he was.

"Please tell me you've decided to call this off, Rei," he said.

"I can't, Hauser. That amulet was taken from a witch coven a century ago. It ended up in the hands of a private collector until he died, and his family donated it. It's supposed to summon your ancestors. We've hit a dead end looking into my background. I need to know how I ended up here instead of in Hell with my family."

"We should have found a witch when we still had the chance," Hauser growled. "You wouldn't have even been thinking about this if we summoned another demon and just asked."

"Yeah, but someone set fire to all the greenhouses that grew what they needed to do that and destroyed all the seeds. The only people that would have reason to do that are demons. I don't think they like being summoned. One of them could have killed all of us."

"Not you. They wouldn't have killed you, Rei. I would

gladly die for you to get your answers and *not* rob that museum."

"No! I don't even want to think about you dying. I won't get caught, Hauser. You taught me well. I've been casing the place for three weeks. I know how to get in and out, and I know how to disable their security without them knowing."

"This is a bad idea, Rei. What are you going to do with it after you have it? You can't keep it at your place when you're done with it. You know better than to have stolen goods at your place. You can't sell it either because this is going to make the news. Covens everywhere got upset when it was taken from the witches and into the hands of that collector. Do you know what would happen if you started approaching covens to sell it to them? They'd come at you to get it from you. They'd rat you out in an instant over that artifact if it meant getting their hands on it."

"I know the risks, Hauser. I'll find someplace to hide it that doesn't lead back to me."

"If you pull this off, the supernatural community will know. There are only four thieves out there that could pull this off. I'll protect you, but you know the other two. They'll rat us out."

I just laughed. I'd thought of that part too. I'd planned this down to a T.

"Yeah, but one of those thieves is a witch without a coven. They'll go to Venus long enough for me to contact my ancestors and get it somewhere safe."

Hauser sighed.

"Put your demon side away for a minute. I taught you better than that. I know we don't like Venus, but you know what they will do to her before they give up it wasn't her, right?"

"She has it coming after what she did to you when you took that job together. She stole all the money, you nearly got caught, and she stole the loot for another buyer, leaving you with a pissed off client after your hide. You got your ass beat by an entire clan of Vampires three times. I give zero shits about sending angry witches after her. She earned it when she betrayed you."

"Do you remember how I stopped you when you wanted to visit her and beat her ass? I'm hoping to do that now."

"Will you just trust me, Hauser? I've planned everything. I won't get caught. Nothing about this will tie back to me. I even have my hiding place planned after I do the ritual. You taught me well. Trust me that I can handle this."

"Fine, Rei. I'll support you on this because I know how much you want these answers. Promise me after this, it's business as usual. No more stealing unless it's for someone else."

"Pinky swear, Hauser."

"Do you need any help? You usually don't anymore, but the stakes are higher this time."

"Come over with a beer and celebrate with me when I get home? If all goes as planned, I'll be back at two in the morning."

"I'll even cook you a steak like old times."

I groaned. Hauser did amazing things to meat. This was it. Tomorrow, I was getting that amulet and finding out why humans raised me.

REI

It was time. I didn't have any family to teach me this. Hauser and I had to figure it out on our own. It took ages, but I learned how to open portals. That was Hauser's rule number six. Plan your transportation in a way that can't be tied back to you. No public transit and don't use your own vehicle. Cameras were everywhere now, and they could track license plates and cars. Hauser got to the mark by his wolf. If we needed to go to another country to steal, well, we both had safes with fake passports for that.

The Museum of the Profane had the best security probably in the entire world. It had never been successfully robbed before, and there was a ton of good shit in there that the supernatural community would have wanted to get their hands on. With all the goodies in here, I was shocked it didn't get broken into more. I couldn't be the only one who wanted something from here, and it wasn't like the Library of the Profane where they would let me use it if they granted me a library card. All these fantastic relics were behind glass cases, and no one could use them anymore. Honestly, some of them were dangerous, and I got why they were on display now, but some of them should have been back with their people.

My portal opened into an air vent above the central security office. It was super cramped, but Hauser didn't sometimes call me runt for no reason. It was a tight fit, but I could do what I needed here. Hauser opened up an entire world for me when he told me I wasn't just a fox shifter. Some shit that always seemed to happen around me started making sense.

Five monitors were watching the museum, and two guards were watching. We weren't totally sure, but I *had* to be a Kitsune after Hauser put me through some intense training. I couldn't just open portals like a demon. I had some pretty fierce magic too. I hadn't even scratched the surface of it either.

Both guards had coffee cups in front of them. I didn't have to spy on them before tonight to know anyone working the night shift staring at screens all night would have coffee or tea at their desks. Trickery was my specialty. I twirled my finger and dropped a little sleeping magic in their coffee. One sip and they'd be out.

It was just a waiting game. Hauser taught me well. No evidence and don't get caught. My visage could not get captured on those cameras. Those computer science classes that bored me to death before I dropped out of college to apprentice with Hauser continued to pay off when it came to security cameras.

Luckily, both guards reached for their coffee at the same time, so shit didn't get awkward when just one of them fell asleep. They both went night-night, and I snuck out of my hiding place. Hauser's little network was vast, and he didn't just teach me himself. He had a Vampire hacker in his employ because sometimes stealing things involved hacking. And I learned more about getting into security systems.

I hopped into the security room to put my next plan in place. I needed to run the cameras on a loop and disable the alarms on the amulet's glass. Easy peasy. Something caught my eye—movement on one camera. No one was supposed to be here. The armed guards didn't patrol the museum unless someone up here pushed a silent alarm. They didn't want their shit getting broken unless it was in danger.

A woman in all black was making a beeline for *my* amulet. I knew that walk. Venus was here stealing my shit, and I was doing all the work for her. Fucking bitch. I was getting that amulet, and Venus was going down for it. I owed her for what she did to Hauser. Let the cameras capture her stealing it. I'd get it from her on the way out.

I hopped back into the air vent and closed the grate. I had to ease myself into the portal I made and ungracefully fall behind some bushes in the parking lot. I felt my body tingle and shrink as I turned into my silver fox. My vision and hearing were always amplified like this, and so was my sense of smell. There was only one exit Venus could take if she didn't want to get caught since she couldn't portal like me, and she was too careless to disable any security. I had a brief window to steal my amulet from her before the armed guards in the museum came spilling into the parking lot, even if the men watching the cameras were now sleeping. The Museum of the Profane took security seriously, which was why no one had successfully stolen from them before.

The alarms were all silent. It didn't matter what they placed it on. The museum didn't want you to know you'd tripped one until security was there with a gun in your face. Venus had to know that. She would have long ended up in jail by now if she was that inept at stealing things. I was dying to know how she intended to pull this off disabling nothing in the control room. I wanted to sneak in there and watch what she was doing, but I also enjoyed my freedom enough not to go down with her if she got caught.

I hoped she had a plan because if she never made it out of the museum with the amulet for me to steal it from her, they were going to up security on it or move it somewhere out of the public eye. It would be a nightmare trying to steal it again after that.

Venus came streaking out of the museum right where I thought she would. My fox was fast. I darted out of the bushes and latched my teeth on her ankle. She tried to kick me off, but I just bit her harder.

"Shit, you're going to get me arrested!"

I just needed her to drop her loot, and that was my plan. Venus would end up in jail for what she did to Hauser and trying to bitch her way into my heist.

"Go away. I got here first!"

I'd made so many mistakes. I'd broken several of Hauser's rules when I realized Venus was here. I felt a pinch in my hindquarters right as Venus went down, and I realized I also broke rule three—always watch your six. As my vision started going black, I heard the pounding of boots and saw men standing over me.

"Are they still offering that reward for the Silver Fox? I think we got a two for one special here, boys."

Shit. If they could tie every single heist to me, I was never getting out of prison. I couldn't even fight because of the dart they hit me with.

I blacked out.

REI

Jail sucked, and they wanted to put me on trial as fast as possible. That boded well for me. The more they rushed to have some circus of a trial because they finally caught me, the less time they had to gather evidence. They saw me at the scene biting Venus, but they found the amulet in her pocket. I already knew they would have clipped my fur at the scene to compare it to the hair I left behind on accident. At most, they could tie me to a five-million-dollar theft and being at the scene of another. I was still going to prison, and there was no avoiding that, but maybe I wouldn't die in there.

They'd pin me with grand theft, and they might even charge me for assaulting Venus, but if they could only pin me at two scenes of crimes, I'd spend a few years in jail and have a release date. I'd do my time, rebuild my reputation, and make sure no one could pin a crime on me again. I could have pulled this off if Venus hadn't ruined everything.

They were holding me in a magical prison before my

trial. I probably could have escaped from a human prison if given enough time, but I wasn't even going to try here—too many variables and too many things that could go wrong. Slipping out with human guards would have been hard, but I could have managed. Sneaking out with a supernatural staff that had so many ways of tracking me? I wasn't stupid. They would kill me.

They had frozen all my assets that they knew about, and I wasn't about to let them know about my offshore accounts. The only reason I had a talented lawyer instead of a public defender was because of Hauser. They wouldn't let him visit, and they weren't allowing me to use the phones to call him.

They had me isolated from the rest of the prison population, and it was driving me insane. I had no one to talk to. The guards were grumpy fucks and wouldn't chat with me. My lawyer didn't like me, and I didn't like her much either, but I was desperate for her visits just to talk with someone.

She sat across from me, looking down at me through her glasses.

"I had to work for this since they want to make an example of you. The theft where you left the hair behind rocked the entire supernatural community. I hope it was worth it. They wanted a big spectacle of a trial that was televised, but I've talked them down from that if you cooperate. I've reminded them they can only technically tie you to one theft, and even though you were at the scene, the amulet wasn't found on your person. I've ironed out a plea deal. You can avoid being paraded around in handcuffs and a public trial if you'll agree to it."

"I'm listening."

"They tore your entire apartment apart and couldn't find anything linking you to crime. Your bank accounts are reasonable for someone running a soap business online. They know if they try to nail you to anything else, it won't stick because there's no proof. I'd say you were an excellent criminal if you weren't caught mauling a witch over something she just stole. They want to nail you for every theft that has happened in the supernatural community, but they can't.

"There's also the issue that the witch you bit was the one who did the stealing. That opens up a whole new can of worms. They are offering a plea deal. Confess to what they can tie you to and tell them where the Destruction Grimoire you stole is, and you'll get seven years in Silverhold Detention Center for the Magically Delinquent. They wanted to tie you to everything and throw you in Scorchwood to rot, but until they finish upgrading it, all the nasties that were in there are currently in Silverhold."

Well, shit. I was a criminal and a thief, but I wasn't a snitch. If I ratted out a client, I'd never be able to show my face in the supernatural community as a thief again. Besides, I didn't know. The whole reason people came to me was anonymity.

"I couldn't tell you where the Grimoire was if I wanted to. I stole it for an anonymous buyer. I never met them in person, even when it was exchanging hands."

Adina looked wholly irritated with me for not ratting out my client. That was the entire purpose of my online store and why people trusted me. It was one of Hauser's rules—they don't know my name, and I needed to do everything I could not to get theirs. Just because I wasn't a snitch didn't mean the people I stole for weren't. If they got caught with my loot, they'd sell me out as the one who did the deed stealing it if it meant a lesser sentence. Hauser and I had a lot more honor as thieves than the people who paid us to steal shit.

"It would really help if you could get that Grimoire back, Rei. The coven you stole it from is wealthy and has the means to make your life very difficult."

I just shrugged.

"It's a Grimoire. I wouldn't have stolen it if another coven hadn't wanted it. They should look at other witches."

Adina pinched the bridge of her nose.

"The witch population is enormous. You were the one that left hair and stole the thing, so they are mad at you. Is there anything you can give me to bring back to make this plea deal work?"

"I'm not a rat, Adina. All I know is that they asked me to steal it, so I did. Since it's a Grimoire, it stands to reason it was witches that asked me. Based on my research of the Grimoire before I took the job, it's got some specific spells in there that I wouldn't be able to cast since I'm not a witch. If they want to find out who has it, track the magic. They do know I'm not a witch, right?"

"That's why it was so upsetting to everyone. A fox shifter stole a powerful Grimoire from an ancient coven of witches, and no one could understand why. Did you even know what that Grimoire could do when you took the job?"

They didn't know. I was in a magical prison, and they all still thought I was a fox shifter. I wasn't about to correct them. Demons rarely came to Earth, and no one knew why. Someone set fire and destroyed the only means to force a demon to appear. It stood to reason the magical community did some awful shit to demons. Hauser met one, and he told me to guard this secret with my life. I wasn't about to correct her. I still didn't know how I ended up here with human parents, but I'd never met another demon in my entire life. I wasn't about to spill that, even to my lawyer.

I just shrugged. I knew exactly what was in that Grimoire. I didn't take just any job. Some things needed to stay where they were, and I didn't steal everything I was asked to.

"The Aether Circle was using it to cause natural disasters so they could get richer. Did they tell you that when they were getting all butt hurt I stole from them? Maybe it's in better hands now."

Adina just glared at me.

"You'd better hope I can work this plea deal because if we have to go to trial, a prosecutor is going to have a field day with you. I think the only thing you're sorry about is getting caught," she said, storming out.

Well, yeah. I was fucking pissed about getting caught. I should have just left instead of trying to get the amulet off Venus in the parking lot. Thinking back, I should have only followed her and stole it much later.

I regretted nothing about all the shit I'd stolen.

REI

It was always nice to have a Vampire in your pocket, even if they couldn't stand you and thought you were an awful criminal. Adina might have wanted to heave me in jail and throw away the key, but she was being paid to make sure I spent as little time behind bars as possible. And she was effective.

Hauser's training had a lot to do with that. If I hadn't shed that one hair stealing the Grimoire, all they could have nailed me with was assaulting Venus, and I totally would have lied through my teeth about seeing her running from the museum, and I was only trying to stop her from getting away. I regretted that damned hair way more than I regretted stealing.

Still, Adina did some kind of Vampire lawyer magic and got my plea deal, despite everyone wanting that fucking Grimoire back. She kept telling me how much the supernatural community wanted me to pay for all their thefts, but some of those weren't even me. Hauser did some of them, and so did Venus. I'd never met them, but others in the thieving business took more jobs than I did. I wasn't asked to rat on them, as if I ever would.

Seven years in Silverhold was a long time, but I could do this. I'd keep my head down, serve my time, and be back to thieving in no time. I kept telling myself that, but honestly? I'd never been terrific about staying out of trouble. Stealing kept my more mischievous side in check, and prison was going to challenge the shit out of me. I was going insane in solitary. I was actually looking forward to Silverhold because I hoped it meant more than four stone walls and no one to talk to.

My transport day had arrived. Adina got my plea deal pushed through pretty quickly, but I was still in solitary for months because they wanted to nail my ass for every little thing that went missing. They didn't work out that plea deal with Adina until they were sure the public wouldn't have gotten all kinds of satisfaction watching me sweat in court for everyone who thought I was the one that stole from them.

Nine months in solitary while they tried to figure that shit out was cruel and unusual punishment. They wouldn't even bring me books when I asked, and I was sure I was going to go crazy if I stayed here longer.

The day had finally come for my transfer. I'd heard nasty things about Silverhold. It was supposed to be a step up from Scorchwood, but still shitty. Prison wasn't supposed to be a vacation, but still, I knew a few people who went out and broke the law just to get arrested because they liked it better than living on the outside. Still, they tried to avoid Silverhold and Scorchwood.

I jumped up when I heard my door unlock. I was desperate for contact at this point. The guard just glared at me.

"Place your hands against the wall and spread your feet."

Another damned frisk? These guards were so fucking pat-down happy. What could I possibly have in here with me? They wouldn't give me anything to pass the time, and they made damned sure they took everything when they fed me. They had tossed my cell several times and were super interested in the toothbrush they gave me.

"I don't have anything on me. I've been begging for something to read for months now."

"Are we going to have a problem, inmate?"

"You literally just tossed my entire cell two days ago."

He shoved me into the wall so hard all the air flew out of my lungs.

"Shut the fuck up. Silverhold will take care of that mouth of yours."

He was clearly not a conversationalist. I didn't want to talk to him anyway, even if I was desperate to speak to someone. I let him do his pat-down, and he snapped chains around my hands and feet. I stumbled as he yanked me out the door. This motherfucker right here was acting like I'd stolen from him personally. I struggled as he pulled me out of my cell.

They were pulling someone else out at the same time. I lost it and went for her eyes when I realized it was Venus.

"Bitch!" I hissed.

"Shifter whore!" Venus yelled.

We both moved to attack each other. She might have blamed me for getting caught, but her sloppy theft job would have done that on its own. I just slowed her down and got myself caught. If she had just stayed away, neither of us would be in jail right now.

I almost had her when my entire body seized. Venus went rigid at the same time. They fucking *shocked* us with their batons. I was so offended by that. Each guard slung one of us over their shoulder and started marching us down the hall.

"Let Silverhold deal with these two," a guard growled.

How was I supposed to keep my head down and not get my sentence extended if fucking *Venus* was going to be there with me? She was going to try to make me pay for getting caught.

And honestly? She needed to pay for me getting caught too.

REI

Seeing as how I'd just spent nine months in solitary and was going to another jail for seven years, I wanted to enjoy as much of the trip as possible. The guards had other ideas. I guess they didn't trust Venus and me together in the back of a transport van. I could behave myself, but I knew Venus couldn't. They ended up drugging both of us, so I couldn't enjoy the fresh air while I could.

When I finally woke up, they strapped me to a table with a woman glaring down at me.

"Good. You're finally awake, and we can get started."

"They didn't have to drug me," I groaned, trying to sit up.

"You broke into a heavily guarded coven compound and stole and highly valuable Grimoire. The witch being transported with you was tied to at least ten high profile thefts at her trial. Like anyone was going to leave the two of you conscious in a transport van and let you escape."

Well, that was just music to my ears. I was still mad

about being drugged and having to go to prison, but Venus wasn't as good a thief as she always bragged about if they tied her to ten other thefts. I was stuck here for seven years, but Venus was going to be here much longer. She deserved it for what she did to Hauser. She begged for his help on that job, then betrayed him. He was the one that was nearly caught when her plan went ass up, and she told him a Vampire clan wanted the loot. Hauser was the one they kept coming after and beating when she stole it for a secondary buyer no one knew about.

"This is the part where I take your blood to key your cuffs, but you're probably the most famous fox shifter here. I just processed another fox for arson, so I'll spare you the needle prick. I can key your cuffs like I did his."

I hid my smile and just nodded. I *did not* want any of these people in Silverhold to know the truth about what I was. Hauser said to keep it a secret, and this would die with me. As much as I wanted to find out more about my heritage, the only people I felt safe asking were Hauser and other demons. I loved it when laziness and loopholes benefited me. If I had to leave something behind, I was glad it was a fox hair because I didn't want anyone in this prison knowing the truth.

The doctor was hunched over a table for a while. She wasn't chatty either. Was there something so wrong about showing criminals a little kindness and talking to them? She turned back to me with two glowing bracelets.

"Silverhold 101. These cuffs are going to suppress your magic. You won't be able to shift. It's the same for everyone in prison. Remotes control the cuffs. If you act out, all they have to do is press a button, and you'll get a shock that disables you. Mouth off, and you'll probably get a jolt. Once a week, you will be allowed yard time where the cuffs are disabled. You can shift and run. You'll only be allowed in the yard with other shifters. Each group gets their own yard time cuff free to do their magic.

"No one wanted this, but some prison rights activists fought for it, so we allow it. If any group fucks this up, we can easily take it away again and say it wasn't working. We can also track you by these cuffs, so don't even think about trying to escape. Our guards have their own supernatural means of tracking besides the cuffs, but if they lose track of you, the cuffs will locate you in an instant. Understand?"

"That's a shitty pep talk, doc."

"No one cares about your feelings here, inmate. Get used to it. I'm going to put the cuffs on. You'll feel them drain your magic as soon as they are closed. Get used to it. You'll only get it back during your yard time."

She closed the bracelets around my wrist, and I didn't feel any magic drained. I had to stop myself from straight-up laughing and giving myself away. Demons had spent so much time away from Earth, I didn't think there were any in Silverhold. They weren't even entertaining the notion I was a Kitsune. Were they rare or something?

Still, I didn't want them to know that. I'd especially take it since they keyed these cuffs for shifters and not demons. I hadn't tested it, but I could still feel my fox and every single ounce of my magic.

I could have some fun with this and make sure Venus didn't come near me for my seven-year stint here.

Another guard came in and glared at me.

"Welcome to Silverhold, cupcake. Now that your magic has been neutered, I'll be bringing you to your cell."

I just smiled sweetly.

"Can't wait."

FAUST

New inmates were a dime a dozen and didn't interest me, but it wasn't every day I was to be CO to someone on that many most-wanted lists. If you were evil enough to be that wanted, they usually threw you straight in Scorchwood. I tried to get on as a guard there, but nothing I tried could even get me a fucking interview. After it hit the news the Warden of Scorchwood was corrupt, it made sense. She wanted criminals as guards. She could have had one, but I didn't leave evidence, so I didn't look good on paper to her. It was pretty fucking ironic I was lording over all these criminals in Silverhold when I should have been here right behind bars with them.

I could smell the Silver Fox before I saw her. My wolf let out this little growl. I knew fox shifters. I'd hunted and killed a few of them. And she wasn't even remotely a fox shifter. My curiosity was definitely piqued. I'd followed the news when it broke they had caught her. She left a silver hair behind at a crime scene that was identified as a fox. They clipped her hair when they knocked her out at the scene before she shifted back and compared them—same fox.

I was a shifter, even if I was superior to a fox. *No one* in the supernatural community left hair behind of an animal unless they were a shifter. Witches had been trying to figure out how to assume animal form for ages. At most, they had familiars. That fox wasn't her familiar because they had caught her shifted.

I knew my nose. The Silver Fox *was not* a shifter. Color me curious. She just got a million times more exciting, and whatever she was, it smelled good to my wolf. It smelled a little like prey, but prey that would make the hunt a lot of fun.

I perked right up when she came into view. Yes, I was definitely hunting this creature in Silverhold. She was tiny and maybe one hundred pounds soaking wet. The Silver Fox had skin the color of coffee with a lot of cream and beautiful almond-shaped eyes. Her long hair was pure white, and I could tell her eyes were violet. She definitely wasn't a shifter. I'd met Japanese shifters before, and they looked nothing like her.

She was fucking gorgeous, and my cock stirred at the idea of stalking her through this prison. I rarely got turned on by my prey, but most of them weren't that pretty. Still, I wouldn't kill her unless someone paid me to. I had this job for a reason. Sometimes, people didn't think jail was enough for criminals. I was a trained assassin, but after I left my pack, I had specific rules about the jobs I took.

My old pack killed anyone they were asked to kill. I was raised since I was a pup to do the same. My pack didn't care about feelings or what children might need. I had alpha blood, so they shipped me off to apprentice with our pack alpha. I was beaten and molded until I became the perfect killer. My alpha fully intended for me to challenge him in a fight and take over for him.

But I wasn't stupid. Everyone liked to pretend shifters were slaves to their instincts, and wolves were beholden to the moon. I made my own decisions. I was a slave to no one, and nothing made me do something I didn't want to do. And I had issues killing people who didn't have it coming.

I broke away from my pack after a massive argument with my alpha about a kill they had approached us about. I had a big fucking problem with it. Some witches wanted us to kill their human neighbor because he played his music too loudly, and it was disturbing their chanting. Honestly? I could have roughed up the neighbor a little and gotten him to stop. I didn't need to make him dead just so some witches could have some peace and quiet.

That was what I wanted to do, but my alpha kept insisting they wouldn't pay us as much if we didn't kill him. That was when I was done. There needed to be a line somewhere over who assassins killed. Were we just going to start taking people out because their dog shit on your lawn? It was annoying, but beating people could be just as effective.

I stepped out on my own and got my name out. I only took the jobs I wanted to take. And it usually involved killing bad people. Sometimes, the problem was they got caught before I could get a bullet in their head or rip their throat out with my teeth. Getting a job in Silver-hold was so much easier. It was like shooting fish in a barrel. There were plenty of wolves in here for murder I could blame it on too.

The Silver Fox had pissed many people off, but no one wanted her dead as far as I knew. Hunting for fun was still fun, and I intended to do that all over this prison until I figured out exactly what the pretty little thing was.

Because I liked the way she smelled, and the hunt was officially on. She just didn't know it.

I hadn't gotten to the actual prison part of Silverhold, but I was following this guard, thinking I had pretty enormous balls knowing these handcuffs didn't take away my magic. I could defend myself if Venus or anyone else came at me. I was telling myself I could do this, and it wouldn't be that bad. I could deal with seven years as long as they didn't put me back in solitary. I had a feeling I was in there the first time because of Venus, and she had to deal with it too.

All my bravado melted away when I was led to a metal door, and a massive wolf was standing there. I could tell he was an alpha too. Hauser told me all about alpha wolves. I was supposed to avoid them at all costs. I usually avoided shifters in general, so they didn't scent my secret. And this fucking wolf was looking at me like I made him curious. Note to self, avoid him at all costs.

"Inmate, this is CO Faust. He's going to be responsible for you doing your stay. You won't get jack shit in here unless you earn it, but you can always ask him for something if you think you have."

Faust's amber eyes glittered, and he grinned at me. Even if I hadn't been told to stay away from alphas, that smile was dangerous. He was way too interested in me as an inmate, and that was the smile of a killer. I stopped dead in my tracks. It was only my first day, but did they let you swap COs if yours was crazy?

Faust stalked over to me and yanked my chains. He also *sniffed my hair.* Because that wasn't creepy. And he growled at me. I was pressed right up against his chest as he frog marched me through the door.

"I know you aren't a simple fox shifter," he growled in my ear. "You might fool everyone in here, but I'm going to find out the truth, little prey."

"I've never been to prison before, but I'm pretty sure guards aren't supposed to hunt inmate, asshole."

He just chuckled and dug his fingers into my arm.

"If it's a good hunt, no one knows about it. I only gave you the heads up to make it more fun. Rat me out, and I'll tell them they need to take a harder look at your cuffs. Doctor Cromwell is nothing if predictably lazy, and we just took in a fox shifter. Let me guess, she skipped the blood test and just keyed the cuffs the same as our latest fox."

This guy right here. If he knew my cuffs weren't keyed right, why wasn't he ratting me out? He said he didn't know what I was, but I guess he thought he was superior enough to whatever it was that he could handle me with my magic. What an arrogant fuck. I was a thief, not a killer, but I would defend myself if he wanted to make my stay here for some fucked up hunting game.

"You probably deserve to be in here more than I do," I hissed as he dragged me down a long hallway.

"Maybe. But I wouldn't be caught dead biting the

ankle of a witch at the scene of a crime. If she had something I wanted, I would have gone for her throat before anyone could get a dart in me. If you had just killed her, you wouldn't be here right now and would be off with your loot."

"You're psycho. Don't they have some kind of psychological test of this job before they let you in here? I steal. I don't kill."

"Grow up, cupcake. You're in prison now. You'd better get good at killing if you intend to keep up your little stealing habit in here. They might not have magic here, but every time we toss cells, we find homemade weapons. You'll get shanked with a toothbrush if you try stealing from people in here."

Was it wrong that just made me want to try it more? The stakes were higher. Could I steal from other thieves and murderers?

"If I get caught."

Faust roughly pulled me to his chest and growled at me again.

"This is prison. You *will* get caught. People will rat you out for a pack of cigarettes or toilet hooch. I have a vested interest in keeping you alive until I find out what you are. After that, I don't care if you take a shank to the gut in the middle of the night because you stole someone's commissary cookies."

Well, prison just got even more fucked up. I thought I'd be avoiding Venus and Scorchwood killers. I now had a psycho guard who was playing a sick game to find out what I was. Hauser told me all about wolf hunts. It wasn't just stalking. A lot of it was psychological. Faust was in a position of power here and could make things a lot more difficult for me here.

"I know exactly what I am."

Maybe if I just told him, I could avoid all this.

Faust slammed me against the wall and pressed his finger to my lips.

"Shh, princess. I don't want you just to *tell* me. There's no fun in that. If you tell me before I break you, a little hunt will seem like a dream vacation compared to what I do to you after that. Don't ruin this for me. I've marked you as prey, but I don't intend to kill you just yet. Let me have my fun. You may enjoy it."

I already knew I wasn't going to enjoy a fucking thing about an alpha hunt that involved me. I fucked up, trying to take the amulet from Venus in the parking lot. I thought I just needed to keep my head down and serve my time.

I knew Venus would be after me, but Faust, who was supposed to be here to protect me, now was too.

We needed a thief. And a good one to boot. Just our luck, a pretty damned famous one was moving into the cellblock next door. I hoped we could trust her. Rajack and I had been serving life in Scorchwood together. We were cellmates and wouldn't have dreamed of trying to break out. It was supposed to be impossible. There was this Vampire there named Roman, who got out the front door a few times, but they always caught him. Whatever they did to him after they brought him back one time turned him into this crazy motherfucker.

But Silverhold? We had a lot more freedom here than we did at Scorchwood. And tasting a few comforts had us wanting more. We wanted out. I was a sphinx, and Rajack was a gargoyle. They threw me in Scorchwood to rot for selling on the black market. The prison term for that in Egypt now was ten years. But did anyone let me out? No. I'd long served my time several times over.

Rajack killed a pedophile. They should have given him a medal after what he told me he caught the guy doing. Apparently, even rich perverts had families that loved them, despite being deviant. They made sure he got sent to Scorchwood for life.

We were done. We survive the frigid temperatures, shitty conditions, killers, rapists, and psychos in Scorchwood. We served our time. We couldn't file for any type of appeal in Scorchwood. We didn't even have a library in there. Silverhold had books and computers, but those of us left to rot in Scorchwood didn't even know what a fucking computer was, much less how to use one to get ourselves out of jail.

Rajack and I figured out the magic box long enough to start the process of an appeal, but we'd been waiting for months for a reply, and we were done. We were breaking out. We just needed a thief we could trust. I was good at selling stolen goods, but I wasn't good at stealing them myself.

Oh, fuck. I got my first look at the Silver Fox when she got dragged in by Faust. Faust was the evilest CO in the entire prison. We all knew he was killing prisoners, but we didn't have a shred of proof. And no one was about to bring that shit up to the warden without it because Faust would just kill you next.

I so didn't need Faust's attention on my thief, and based on how he wasn't even trying to hide it, he was super interested in her. He finally got his big ass, bulky wolf frame out of the way so I could see her. Oh! She was so tiny and pretty! I wanted to keep her when we got out. We'd have to find a safe place to live once we were wanted fugitives. Color me curious about this fox.

I snarled when Faust roughly shoved her in her cell and threw her bag of prison essentials at her face. That was *my* thief. No one was allowed to touch her, not even fucking Faust. He whispered something in her ear and stalked off to do whatever psycho COs do when they aren't murdering inmates. I slipped into her cell all sly like.

"Well, hello there. I've been wanting to meet you. I've been following you on the two magic boxes the prison offers."

She cocked an eyebrow at me.

"Magic boxes?"

"The television and computer. They didn't have those in Scorchwood. We didn't even have books. Dreadful place. Some of us who transferred here are seeing a brand new world of things we didn't know existed."

She visibly recoiled when I mentioned my previous stint was in Scorchwood. That was to be expected. All the bad people ended up in Scorchwood unless some palms were greased or you really offended someone. The Egyptian government had always hated the black market and tried to shut it down. It wasn't usually a Scorchwood sentence, though. They thought making an example of me would deter people. It didn't.

I held up my hands.

"I was there for trading much needed medical supplies to hospitals on the black market because they couldn't get them from the government or anywhere else. There was a virus spreading around Egypt, and hospitals and medical clinics didn't have the things they needed to treat people. I got them those things. They made an example of me to discourage the whole black market by sending me to Scorchwood. My cellmate in Scorchwood is here too. They gave him life for killing a pedophile he caught in the act."

She wrinkled her nose in confusion.

"Why'd they throw him in Scorchwood for that?"

"The pedophile came from a rich family, and they tried to make the argument he was unarmed and could have been subdued. There were some bad people in Scorchwood, and there are some bad people here, but they can all agree you don't hurt kids. If you end up in jail for doing that, you aren't going to have a good time of it."

"I guess you know I'm here for theft, then. Rei Anderson," she said, holding out her hand.

"Dakarys El Sadat. I'm a sphinx. Rajack is a gargoyle, but he's not here right now. He's checking his appeal on the magic box. We both desperately want to get out of here."

Baby steps. I needed her, but I needed to know we could trust her. Trusting people was hard in prison. We were all criminals, after all. I couldn't just dump an entire escape plan on her right when we first met. I didn't know who *wouldn't* want to break out of here, but I needed to know she wasn't a snitch. She could rat us out to get a few years knocked off her sentence.

She sighed and slumped against the wall.

"So do I, but I don't think it's going to happen. They totally wanted to nail my ass for everything that's ever been stolen, but they couldn't link me to anything except one theft and being at the scene of another. I thought if I kept my head down, I might get off early on exemplary behavior, but Faust has taken an interest in me."

I grabbed her hand and squeezed it. I did *not* need Faust killing my thief. Everyone knew better than to attract his attention.

"Stay away from Faust at all costs. He's dangerous."

"What's the deal with him? I got that vibe off him."

"No one has any proof because they aren't wolf kills, but three inmates have mysteriously died since Rajack, and I got transferred. People who have been here a while talk. There's been a lot of unexplained deaths since Faust got the job. This place isn't Scorchwood, where there were no guards on the floor, and you had to watch your back because we expected someone would kill you. There's a lot more security here, so inmates don't die. It still happens here. Inmates like to brag. If someone here did it, they would have copped to it for cred with the gangs. If one of the gangs were responsible, they would have said so to make a point with the other gangs. It wasn't anyone here, so it has to be a guard. Faust is the only one who makes people here uncomfortable, and that's saying a lot considering we are all criminals."

Faust flat out gave me the creeps. His hair was black as night, and his beard was just too well-groomed. His amber eyes always seemed to hit the light like his wolf was scratching at the surface to come out and rip throats out.

Rei just smiled at me.

"I've never met a sphinx before. Or a gargoyle for that matter."

I shrugged. That wasn't shocking. She had an American accent.

"We tend to stick to certain countries unless we get arrested and thrown into magical prisons and don't have a choice. I'd like to see my home again, but I doubt that's possible."

Especially if we successfully broke out of Silverhold. I read up on current events in Egypt once I figured out the magic box computer. Things had changed since they arrested me. If I went back, I'd probably end up in jail again, and I never wanted to do that.

Rei looked far away.

"I was adopted. My adoptive parents won't tell me for sure, but I think my family is from Japan. I got to visit on a job, and it was pretty much amazing. If my mentor weren't in the States, I'd move there permanently."

Mentors were never a good thing when you needed a thief to break you out of prison. Especially if they taught you how to commit felonies. There was usually some sort of honor code in there, and I needed Rei to be bad enough to want to break us out. If she was close with her mentor, she might not want to go on the run and actually serve her time here.

The dinner bell started ringing, and she jumped because it startled her. I grabbed her hand and pulled her to her feet.

"That bell means food. It's gourmet compared to Scorchwood food, but it's still shitty. Eat with me. Until Faust gets your commissary up and assigns you a job, it's the only food you'll get."

She let me lead her out of her cell and to the mess hall —step one, complete. Introduce myself to the Silver Fox. Onto step two. Figuring out if I could trust her.

As far as prison friends went, I was glad Dakarys introduced himself. I was wary when he said he transferred from Scorchwood, but after everything that recently hit the news, I wasn't surprised people may have ended up there because money exchanged hands or their government was trying to make an example of them.

It didn't hurt that Dakarys was massive and bloody gorgeous as well. He was easily as big as Faust with bright green eyes, olive skin, a full, kissable mouth, and blond streaks in his black hair that looked natural instead of out of a box.

He was friendly and could probably help me figure out how to survive here with Faust's attention on me. It wouldn't hurt to have a sphinx watching my back with Venus here either. I had a feeling the gangs here went by species, and she was going to rile all the witches and warlocks up here to come at me. She was petty enough to have other witches do her dirty work, so her sentence wouldn't get extended. Because I bit her to steal the amulet, I got caught, but honestly? She would have done that on her own. She didn't disable the security cameras or the alarm and had guards chasing her. They would have caught her before she made it out of the parking lot. I had been hoping to catch her first, and that was my big mistake.

There was nothing I could do about that now. I was in prison. Now, I just needed to make some allies to make sure I survived Venus and Faust. Especially if inmates tended to go missing around him. Venus wouldn't have her magic, and neither would any witches she joined up with. Faust didn't rat me out about my handcuff. He could have easily hauled me back in there and gotten an answer about what I was with a blood test. He was clearly fucked in the head if he wanted to leave me in prison with magic for the shits and giggles of figuring out what I was on his own.

The mess hall was vast, and the line was long. Dakarys pulled me straight to the front and skipped everyone in line. No one beat him or complained. No one said anything about the new girl going directly to the front either. I leaned into him.

"How did you just do that and not get both of us killed?"

Dakarys just smirked at me.

"Computers and television may have been invented while I was rotting in Scorchwood, and I thought they were magic, but they kind of are. We got assigned to the mailroom, and the Silverhold black market is now booming. Honestly, I'm shocked no one pulled it off before I got here. No one lays a finger on Rajack and me because they know we'll cut off their supply of whatever their little black hearts want in prison they can't get at the commissary. Do you want something? Because I can get it."

Well, fuck. Now I was even more grateful Dakarys wanted to be friends. No one would fuck with me except Faust if we made friends. And he was just lovely. I grabbed my tray and started eyeing the food.

"Silverhold 101, Rei. You don't get medical treatment unless it's an emergency. Some food will fuck you up, but you can use it. Stay away from anything with peanut butter in it. You won't shit for days. If you absolutely need it or they are serving a peanut butter dessert, eat something with cheese. I don't care how much you like cheese. You won't like Silverhold cheese. It's bright orange and doesn't taste like normal cheese. If you overeat, you'll be peeing out your ass for days. The meat is all mushy lumps, and they cut it with breadcrumbs to make it go further. It's not properly seasoned, and we have no idea which animal it's from. It's disgusting but eat it anyway. You need protein in here in case anyone comes at you."

My hand paused over the mac and cheese. It was pretty much my favorite food ever because it was hard to mess up. They had fucking weaponized mac and cheese in here to give you the trots, and prison just got a million times worse.

"How much of this can I eat before I have to live in the bathroom?"

Dakarys winked at me.

"A risk-taker. I can dig it. A serving isn't going to do anything to you, but I wouldn't do seconds. If they do peanut butter sandwiches with the mac and cheese, you can eat all you want because they cancel each other out. Sometimes, they give us this peanut butter pie that's not half bad, and it cancels the cheese out too, but they don't set it out often because they know we like it."

This was the grossest looking mac and cheese I'd ever seen in my entire life, which kind of shattered my notion it was an impossible food to fuck up. Even cheap boxed mac didn't look this bad. It made this squelching noise when I dumped it on my plate.

The cheese was this neon orange, but it looked like everything else they were offering us was gray. The mushy peas were gray, and so was the mystery meat. I wasn't the best cook in the world, but I could manage better than this. Still, this was prison, and I knew the food was going to be bad. I spooned some peas and slapped some gray meat on my plate.

Dakarys put his hand over mine.

"Use the gravy on everything. It's the only thing they put seasoning in. It's just salt and pepper, but it's going to save everything on your plate. Grab a pudding too. They hand those out if we don't get something sweet cooked. The pudding is decent, and people have gotten beaten for the butterscotch."

I slipped a pudding on my tray and followed him to a table. No one was sitting there except an utterly beautiful man. His skin was the color of black coffee, and he had silver eyes. He was even bigger than Faust, and he had the top of his jumpsuit off. He was seriously cut in his undershirt, and he seemed to know who I was because he gave me a friendly smile when I sat down.

"I take it you found the Silver Fox?"

"Rei," I said, holding out my hand.

"Rajack. We've been following you on the computer."

Why? I'd never stolen from a sphinx or a gargoyle before. I doubt they gave a shit about that Grimoire or the amulet I was trying to get my hands on. Witches could only use the Grimoire, and witches had created the amulet, but anyone could use it. I couldn't even claim street cred in here for successfully robbing the Museum of the Profane because Venus ruined that.

"I'm just a thief, and I'm sure there are plenty in here. I'm not that interesting."

Rajack just grinned at me.

"The other thieves here are sloppy, and we don't like them. Tell me, why did you bite that witch and get caught?"

I sighed.

"I asked myself that a million times while I was in solitary waiting to be brought here. I was trying to rob the Museum of the Profane, and I had a plan. Venus showed up and ruined it. I had to improvise. I had this vision of biting her, getting the amulet, and leaving her for the guards, but it didn't play out that way. I owed her for betraying my mentor."

"Venus is over there trying to get close to Astrid. Astrid is the high priestess of the witch gang in here, and the witches do nothing without her approval."

My eyes darted across the room. Yeah, there was Venus trying to kiss ass to sit next to a woman with long, black hair. I knew better than to expect Venus not to come at me here. If she were as sloppy as she was at the Museum of the Profane and they linked her to several other thefts, then she would have ended up here eventually, even without me biting her.

"Yeah, that's her. I'm going to have a problem with witches and Faust while I'm here."

Dakarys just smirked.

"We'll watch your back with Faust, but if we claim

you, no witch will touch you. Black market, remember? The witches might not have their magic with those cuffs on, but they can brew some of their potions without it, and they like their talismans. Astrid is fair and smart. She likes her revenge just as much as the next witch, or she wouldn't be here, but she'd not dumb enough to deprive her entire gang of what I could get for them because of one witch."

"I'm not sure I understand why you want to claim me and offer prison protection. I'm not complaining, but why? It can't just be the news stories. They painted me as this horrible person for the things they could nail me with."

It wasn't like I could go to the shifters for protection. Faust was already going to be a problem. I didn't need every shifter in here curious about me. The supernatural community was cliquey. The witches were out because of Venus. The Vampires would only take me if I let them feed on me. There were no other demons in here, or Faust wouldn't be so curious. It would be smart to partner up with Dakarys and Rajack, but that was Hauser's rule six—trust no one until they proved they had earned it.

Dakarys had been helpful about the food and giving me information about Faust. They'd offered to help me with the witches. But what did they want in return? People always wanted something. Being a professional thief was a testament to that. They coveted things so severely, they were willing to pay me a lot of money to steal them.

Dakarys and Rajack leaned in conspiratorially.

"Can we trust you? Like, *really* trust you? Are you a snitch, Rei?"

This was good. We were getting somewhere. They needed to trust me too. I was many things, and I got off on breaking the law, but I *was not* a rat. I was a little offended they asked.

"They tried to offer me a plea deal if I would rat on who I gave the Grimoire to. Even if I knew, I wouldn't have told them. My business ran on anonymity for a reason. I won't sell someone out, but my clients totally would."

Rajack let out a deep chuckle. He had this sexy voice.

"I really don't think you need to worry about your witch friend. We followed her, too, when we knew we had two potential thieves coming. You might not have ratted anyone out, but the witch did. If Astrid finds out she ratted on other witches, she'll banish her from the gang. People get beaten and murdered in here. Shit gets stolen all the time. But one thing is sacred no matter what prison you are in—don't snitch on other inmates."

I threw back my head and laughed. I could handle that, but Venus totally couldn't.

"I'm not a snitch, so why don't you tell me what you think I'll tell on you for?"

Dakarys's eyes glittered.

"We require a master thief. It will be the biggest heist you've ever pulled off and give you a ton of street cred. But we can get to that later. Why don't we all get to know each other first?"

He didn't have to say any more. The biggest heist ever? I was so here for that. The stakes for stealing in prison were so much higher than out in the world.

And I wasn't getting caught this time. The fact that both Venus and Faust would be up my ass while I tried to pull this off just made it a million times more fun.

RAJACK

We had our thief, and I wanted out of here yesterday, but I understood why Dakarys took his time with her. We needed trust all around. If these handcuffs weren't on my wrist, I would have known instantly if she was lying. Gargoyles could always tell if someone wasn't telling the truth. I couldn't interrogate her with my gargoyle gifts until she'd stolen a key to these cuffs, among the other things we needed her to steal for this to work.

Dakarys and I quickly decided we couldn't trust a single thief in Silverhold. They tended to die pretty quickly here because they had sticky fingers and stole from people they shouldn't have. So, we got really interested in the news and who might end up in Silverhold with us.

We perked right the fuck up when two thieves had been arrested outside the Museum of the Profane. It was all over the news because of what they housed there. There were all kinds of dangerous and cursed relics behind those walls, and security was so tight, no one had tried breaking in since before I got arrested.

We had two potential thieves coming with balls big enough to try to break into the Museum of the Profane. I was against the fox at first since she seemed a little bitey, but then it became clear we couldn't use the witch.

We followed both of them closely, trying to determine their methods. We had absolutely no idea how the Silver Fox was breaking in and only left behind one hair. The witch was using her magic, and that could be tracked. She also left an enormous mess behind at every scene. Sloppy. She would have been caught even if the fox didn't slow her down by biting her ankle.

It wasn't even a discussion. Both thieves weren't stealing for themselves. That much became obvious. As evidence started piling up against the witch, arrests started getting made in the supernatural community for the clients who paid her to steal for them. All the loot was recovered, and people ended up in another magical prison besides Silverhold. Silverhold was where the bad people went now that Scorchwood was closed for renovations.

We wanted out of Silverhold, but not enough to trust a sloppy witch who would snitch to save her own ass. It became pretty obvious the Silver Fox was going to be our only option unless another thief got arrested. And it would have to be a significant player to end up in Silverhold. Pickpockets didn't end up here. Usually, people made a mess robbing banks, gas stations, or got caught too many times breaking into houses. And that was not the kind of thief we needed. We needed a *good* thief.

It didn't hurt that she was beautiful. I thought that every time they flashed her mug shot on the news. She managed to look not the least bit sorry in her mug shot. That was another reason I was against using her at first. She was smirking right at the camera, and I just had this feeling they made her retake it because she winked and flipped her middle finger at the camera.

Still, now that I'd met her, I was glad she was here. I knew that Grimoire wasn't the only thing she had stolen. It was just the only scene she'd left evidence behind. She was good, aside from getting sloppy at the museum. I had a lot of questions about that, and we were technically trying to build trust. Why *did* she bite the witch and get caught when she had been so careful before? She could have easily told her client who she stole it for and ruined the job for her instead of getting herself caught.

We were all back in Dakarys and I's cell shooting the shit.

"Fess up, Rei. You were meticulous before if you only managed to leave one of your fox hairs behind. If that witch was stealing your job, why risk everything instead of calling your client?"

Rei deflated.

"Honestly? That job wasn't for a client. I wanted the amulet for me. My mentor tried to talk me out of it. It was one of his rules. Never steal for yourself. I'm adopted, and I wanted to find out more about my past. Humans raised me. I have a lot of questions only my ancestors can answer."

I didn't have to have my gargoyle gifts to know she was telling the truth, but she left something out. Something pretty significant that we probably needed to know. Baby steps. She didn't trust us yet. The feeling was mutual. If she kept this big secret, then I didn't trust her either. No one had ever broken out of Silverhold before.

If we were going to do this, then we all needed to be on the same page. No secrets.

"Did you want me to ask around with the fox shifters here?" Dakarys said. "Maybe we can find out which skulk you came from."

"No!" she said, a little too quickly for me.

Foxes weren't pack animals like a lot of shifters. They stayed in families called skulks. The chances of anyone in her skulk being in Scorchwood were pretty fucking slim, but her white hair and violet eyes marked her as pretty rare for most fox shifters with ancestors from Japan. That had to be talked about somewhere. If she was willing to get herself caught to get that amulet, why didn't she want us talking to the fox shifters? Why was she here with us instead of the other shifters?

I had questions.

"You seem to be avoiding the other shifters. Some drama there?" I asked.

"I was raised with humans. My mentor was a wolf. He always told me to avoid other shifters."

That much was true, but she was leaving something out again. Wolves didn't take foxes in and teach them. They looked down on them as prey. Shifters had a lot a drama with other shifters, and each group thought they were superior in their animal form. Many of them looked down on the foxes, but foxes looked down their noses on some too. A wolf *would never* have taught a fox to steal as well as she did.

"Something isn't adding up, Rei," I said. "A wolf would never teach a fox."

"Do you always judge people by their race? Not everyone is the same. Hauser caught me picking his pocket. He could have killed me, but he chose to teach me instead."

She got angry at that. She wasn't lying, but it didn't make a lick of sense. Every single wolf I'd ever met, and there were plenty in prison, would have killed a fox shifter for stealing from them. I guess it stood to reason this Hauser was different, but she was still leaving something out. Dakarys was trying to smooth things over while ignoring what she was leaving out.

"Hauser sounds like an amazing man, and he clearly taught you well. He must have had his reasons for telling you to avoid other shifters. I won't ask around."

Yeah, clearly. I heard all about how Faust was interested in her. One wolf took her in and taught her, and another wolf was up her ass.

I couldn't smell her like a shifter would, but something told me there was more to Rei than just a simple fox shifter. And I didn't know if I could trust that.

REI

I didn't currently have a cellmate, and I didn't know how I felt about that. On the one hand, I enjoyed talking, and it wouldn't hurt to have someone watching if Venus turned her toothbrush into a shank and came in here to stab me. On the other, I could pick which bunk I wanted. Both of them were pretty fucking uncomfortable.

Faust didn't say a damned thing to me when he came down to do a headcount to make sure everyone was in their cells and lock us in for the night, but he sure sniffed the air a lot, and his amber eyes never left me until he had to leave to go to another cell. I didn't mind being locked in. I wanted a locked door between Venus and her toothbrush. I didn't like being locked in knowing Faust had a key.

I liked Dakarys and Rajack, but they asked me more questions than I got to ask them. Rajack knew I was leaving things out and didn't trust me as much as Dakarys did, but until he started answering some of my questions, I didn't trust him much either.

I knew I needed to. Hauser said to keep my demon lineage a secret, but I needed help keeping Faust and other shifters away from me. It wouldn't do having the entire prison on some fucked up hunt. I wasn't stupid enough to think I didn't need their help. They needed mine too. We needed trust all around because I had a feeling whatever theft they required me to do was going to be significant.

I managed to get some sleep on the very uncomfortable cot. Being a thief meant I got to sleep in and not have to get up early and go to an office. Why the entire world expected everyone to be morning people was beyond me. Prison was no different. This awful bell started blaring throughout the whole prison, and the lights came on at some dreadful hour I wasn't usually conscious.

I pulled the blanket over my head and intended to ignore it. Someone *ripped my blanket off.* I rolled over, and there was fucking Faust.

"Out of bed, princess. It's time for count."

"Count me from here," I moaned, burying my face in my pillow.

He grabbed my ankle and yanked me out of bed. I hit my funny bone on the edge of the bed as my ass hit the floor.

"Asshole!" I hissed.

"You will get your ass to the front of your cell and stand for count. After that, you will take a shower and get to the mess hall for breakfast. I haven't assigned your work detail yet, so don't get into any trouble with your free time. There's a library with a computer. Why don't you go study how to better yourself when you get out of here?"

"I want to work in the mailroom," I said as I brushed myself off and got to my feet. I was pretty sure he broke my ass, and my funny bone still hurt.

"You'll work where I say you work. I'm your CO. My opinions are your opinions. I own you for the next seven years, inmate. Now, shut up and stand outside your cell."

I hoped that meant I survived the next seven years if what Dakarys said was true about Faust. I hated him, but I didn't want to give him any reason to kill me, so I went and stood outside my cell. My stomach let out this massive rumble as Faust stalked down the hall as slowly as possible, clicking something at all us criminals. Faust finally got to the end of the hall and turned to glare at us.

"I hope you all hit the showers before breakfast. You reek of crime and shame."

Asshole.

I followed the crowd to the showers. I already knew it was a group shower kind of thing, but after living with a wolf, nudity didn't offend me, and I'd never really been ashamed of my body. I shrugged my jumper off and placed it in one of the lockers. There was shampoo and soap in the bag Faust threw at my head, so I carried it with me to the showers.

I was glad I watched my back in the showers. I wasn't worried about the fact that there were naked men here. Hauser taught me how to defend myself against a bigger foe. Venus came strolling into the showers flanked by two witches and zeroed in on me right away.

"Nice tits," she growled.

"Those paper shoes are a huge downgrade from your usual Louboutin's, Venus."

"Bitch!" she shrieked, flying at me.

The one thing that Venus was super sensitive about

was shoes. When Hauser agreed to take that job with her, she always wore these tall heels. The first time she came to his house, she snapped a heel in his kitchen. She pitched this massive fit and got dramatic about it like it was somehow Hauser's fault she stepped wrong.

I ducked as Venus's fist flew at my face. She shrieked when her hand connected with the tile. She brought two witches with her, but they weren't helping her. I could fight Venus off, but I'd have issues fighting off three of them. They were both exchanging looks like they didn't know if they should jump in. The other inmates had formed a circle around us and were chanting. They didn't know either of us to root for either one. They just wanted to see us beat each other up.

Venus tried to grab my long hair. I was a goner if she got ahold of it. My fist darted out and clipped her in the mouth. I laughed and danced around like a boxer.

"That was for Hauser, you double-crossing bitch."

"I'm going to kill you, Rei!" Venus shrieked.

The witches finally stepped in, but not like how I thought. They pulled Venus away from me like I was one of them. How curious.

"Stop it! Astrid didn't approve of this. You can't kill anyone here unless she says so. Do you want to piss off every witch in Silverhold getting on her bad side?"

"I'm only in here because of that stupid fox! She has it coming."

The two witches started dragging her out of the shower.

"It doesn't matter. Everything goes through Astrid."

"Then take me to Astrid right this minute!"

I just laughed and grabbed my towel to dry off. Astrid may decide to risk her access to Dakarys and Rajack's black market and let her come for me, but I doubted it. Venus was going to piss off every witch in here because she wouldn't drop this.

When I went to leave the shower, I realized Faust had been there watching the entire thing go down, and he hadn't stepped in to try to stop the fight that would have happened if those witches hadn't stepped in. I breezed past him.

"Enjoy the show, perv?"

Faust just smirked at me.

"That witch was right about your tits, inmate. Nice," he said, letting out a wolf whistle.

"I hate you."

"Watch your fucking mouth, inmate. I have a vested interest in keeping you alive until I figure out what you are. You're going to need all the help you can get in here if you piss off the witches. I don't want you dead. Yet."

"That's comforting."

"Get to the mess hall, inmate. I'm backed up on paperwork, and I haven't gotten to your commissary yet. It's the only way you're eating until I get around to it."

I stalked off to my locker and started getting dressed. I had a feeling Faust was going to use my commissary as part of this hunt of his, and it could take ages for me to get my funds. Several people in the showers had flip flops. I desperately wanted a pair because the showers were nasty. Venus had witches here she could borrow things from. It looks like she'd wrapped her feet in maxi pads when she tried to assault me in the shower.

If I started growing some sort of fungus on my feet from those showers because Faust was dicking around with my commissary, I was going to be upset.

I'd done a little digging on my not fox shifter. I knew who the witch was who came in the shower to beat her face in. I would have stepped in if it went too far, but I was hoping she'd do something to give me a little hint. Her cuffs were keyed to neutralize a shifter, and she wasn't even remotely close. Whatever she was, she'd still have her magic. I was hoping she'd use a little to hurt the witch.

Whoever taught her to fight trained her well. It just *had* to be a wolf, which raised a lot of questions for me. I knew what she smelled like to other wolves. She smelled fucking delicious, and she didn't have a mark on her like a wolf had claimed her. My big question was, fucking why? She had me all levels of curious.

If I had to kill that witch who was arrested with her, I had no problem with that. No one was paying me to, but I looked into her too so I could figure out why the scene went down, so they were both caught. I totally understood being a criminal with an honor code. That didn't apply to a lot of the prisoners here.

The witch, inmate 775, would have sold anyone out if it bettered her situation. The not fox mentioned someone named Hauser when she punched inmate 775. I'd lay odds that was the wolf who trained her.

Uncultured people thought wolf hunts involved creeping around and sniffing things, but that was totally wrong. It was so much more nuanced than that. There was research involved. I would be digging deep into inmate 898 and relying on every skill I had to find out what she was.

I already decided I wasn't going to kill her. I wouldn't take the job if someone wanted her dead in here either. She was nothing if entertaining. It wasn't just the hunt that made her fun. The other inmates knew better than to mouth off to me. If they saw me coming, they went the other way.

Not this inmate. She told me she hated me right to my face, and she called me a pervert after I complimented her tits. I never said anything nice unless it was deserved, and she did have a nice pair. They were barely a handful and perky. Even the witch saw that.

I was so behind on my paperwork, but the new inmate was consuming all my thoughts. I could see those violet eyes when I was sleeping. I was having fun with this, even if she hated me.

This was a hunt that didn't involve me killing anyone. Sometimes, killing criminals just got old. And I looked into her. They offered her a plea deal just like the witch. She didn't rat anyone out. If another wolf taught her, then maybe she was a criminal with honor, just like me.

Maybe that explained this pull I felt to her. Because I was trying desperately hard to avoid it.

DAKARYS

*R*ei was taking too long to get to breakfast. There was too much at stake with Faust and that witch after her. Rajack went to get her while I fixed a plate for her. I didn't know what her favorite foods were, but I knew what was acceptable to eat here in Silverhold. The powdered eggs were by far superior to the oatmeal, and there was never enough sausage for the entire prison. I grabbed enough for all three of us.

Rei's late appearance made sense when Astrid plopped down at my table and looked utterly put out. I liked Astrid. Out of all the gang leaders here in Silverhold, she was probably the least petty. She was in here for some epic curses cast in revenge, but you could say those people had it coming.

Astrid took care of her witches and made sure none of them did anything to earn more time here. Sure, they killed and got revenge, but they were sneaky about it, and it never pointed back to them. I *did not* want Astrid and her witches focused on my thief.

"Have you claimed the fox you were sitting with at dinner the other day?" she asked.

"Rajack and I both have, and I already know what you're about to ask. We know all about your new witch and the bad blood between the two. We followed both of them on the news after they got busted. Have you looked into Venus at all?"

Astrid shrugged.

"I know she's a thief, and she got caught because your fox assaulted her. We've come at people for less in here. I know she's yours, but she hurt one of mine."

"We don't deny she bit her, but—"

"Venus would have needed stitches if one of the guards at the scene wasn't a warlock and healed her wound before they took her to jail. She has a scar. Your fox left permanent damage on my witch and landed her in jail."

"Your witch was sloppy. If she were good at what she does, the guards wouldn't have chased her into the parking lot where they were fighting. From what the news said, she was sloppy at several other scenes they tied back to her. She sold out her clients for a lesser sentence. Rei didn't do that."

Astrid sighed.

"Venus left that part out. Still, I have to give her something. Rei busted her lip in the shower."

"I think there's part of that story you're leaving out, Astrid."

"Okay, fine. Venus started it. My witches stopped it. Rei got just as nasty with Venus as she did with Rei."

"I get the feeling there's bad blood there that goes beyond the whole Museum of the Profane. They are both thieves. They probably knew each other before that. Rajack is coming with her now. We can ask her."

"Oh, fine. Can I have one of those sausages?"

I smacked her hand away.

"Only if Rei doesn't want them."

Astrid cocked an eyebrow at me.

"You're pretty possessive over the fox. What's going on, Dakarys?"

"Let me worry about it."

Rajack glared at Venus. I knew he didn't entirely trust Rei yet, but she needed time to spill her secrets. I knew she wasn't telling me everything too, but I didn't think she was ready for that yet.

"Control your witches, Astrid," Rajack growled.

Astrid looked longingly at my sausage haul.

"My witches stopped it, but your fox was the one that did the damage."

"I'd do it again," Rei said. "Venus is a shitty person, and she'll stab you in the back the first chance she gets. I speak from experience."

Astrid perked up.

"Tell me all about your experience, Rei."

I realized how much we lucked out deciding against Venus as Rei told us a story about how Venus betrayed her mentor, almost got him arrested, and they beat him several times. I also realized how much more diligent I was going to have to be watching Rei's six. It wasn't just Faust. Venus was probably sharpening her toothbrush as we spoke. Astrid looked disturbed.

"If what you say is true, I don't want her in my coven, but I can't have her as a free agent and stealing my witches."

Rei shook her head.

"She's always been a free agent. Her coven kicked her out. Other covens would ask her to steal for them, but they didn't want her in their ranks. I've dealt with witches before as clients. I won't steal something if I know they are going to use it to cause harm."

"I'm not clueless, Rei. I know about the Grimoire you stole and what it can do," Astrid said.

"Did you know the coven I stole it from was using it to do bad things?"

"She also didn't rat on who she stole it for like Venus did. Venus sent several witches to jail," I said proudly like I'd trained Rei myself.

Rajack had more of an understanding with Astrid than I did. I got the product and moved things around, but Rajack arranged the trades. I'd gotten to know Astrid, but he spent more time with her.

"I know what kind of position this puts you in, Astrid. You can't be seen siding with Rei over Venus, but you also know we'll cut you off so fast if you hurt her. You have to work with Venus, so she doesn't steal your witches. I have an idea."

I loved it when his gargoyle brain started working. Rajack was super intelligent. It was the entire reason we got the computers figured out so fast, and he helped me get our black market enterprise up and running. Whatever he said was going to save Rei from the witches, leaving us to worry about Faust.

"Blame us," Rajack said. "Give them a choice. Tell them you discussed the issue with us, and we told you if any witch came at Rei, your coven won't get any more potion ingredients or talismans. It's the truth. They can have a choice. Revenge or the black market. They don't know Venus all that well yet. They can help Venus and lose their potions, or they leave it."

It was a good idea. It could work. Venus had to want potions too, right? Astrid wouldn't give her ingredients to hurt Rei. Venus had to be feeling the effects of the cuffs by now. It was like a vital part of you had been taken away. I missed my sphinx more than anything. I could access him in Scorchwood. We all had our magic there. Things were better in Silverhold except for these cuffs. That was why we needed Rei, among the other things we needed her to steal.

Rei just shook her head.

"That may work on the coven, but it won't work on Venus. If you tell her no, even if the entire coven backs you, she'll break away and become a free agent again. She did it for years. She'll start whispering in the ears of other witches until a few have defected. She'll have her own gang and try again."

Astrid tossed her blonde hair over her shoulders.

"I trust my witches. If Venus gets banished, she is dead to us. She can whisper, but we won't listen. Let me deal with my witches. I'll handle this. I can't control Venus, but I can handle my coven."

Astrid disappeared, but I didn't feel much better about this after everything I'd learned about Venus. Venus wasn't getting her hands on anything from my black market, but there was plenty of prison provided items she could turn into a weapon.

My thief came with a lot of danger, and I kind of dug it.

No offense to Astrid. She seemed sweet, but if she thought she could control Venus, I had some property that wasn't stolen to sell her. And I was pretty sure some of her witches were psycho enough to join Venus. There were always psychos wherever you went, and this was prison. Everyone was psycho here.

Dakarys seemed to think it was handled. I just shook my head.

"Venus is a thief, remember? She'll either steal from the witches or figure out how your black market works and steal from you. She knows how to work a computer. She could easily order what she needs."

Dakarys and Rajack just laughed.

"Not with us controlling the mailroom. We'll steal from her and give it to Astrid. We have to get to work. Have you been assigned a job yet, Rei?"

"I asked Faust for the mailroom, and he informed me he owned me. He also said he's behind on my paperwork and would eventually get to my commissary. I have a feeling he's going to use that to his advantage."

"What are you going to do with your day?"

I just shrugged.

"Probably use the computer in the library and stay away from some witches."

We said our goodbyes, and I managed to find the library and computers. I meant to email Hauser, but apparently, all forms of email were blocked. They blocked everything except legal sites and sites on how to better yourself. Well, fuck. I guess if it was prison, you couldn't expect to be able to email. I needed to talk to Hauser. Maybe he could help me with Faust. Where the fuck were the phones?

I managed to find a gym and a window leading out to a yard. No one was out there, but I got my own tour of the prison since Faust didn't bother to give me one. I found the phones. Could I call him with my commissary not in? I tried to get him collect. Right when it was about to connect, a big, meaty hand hung up the phone. I looked up, and there was fucking Faust.

"Asshole!" I hissed.

"Time for work, inmate. I've figured out what your job is going to be."

"The mailroom?" I asked, hopefully.

"Fuck no. Hurry up and follow me."

Faust was huge and walking quickly. I had issues keeping up with him. He opened a door and let me into an office with papers stacked everywhere.

"What the fuck is this?"

Faust leaned back in his chair and stuck his hands behind his head.

"You're going to help me with my paperwork. I told the warden you needed a job, and I needed some help. If you get to the file with your commissary, you can have a cookie. Literally. You'll have your funds and can buy yourself some Oreos."

"You're such an asshole. I *hate* paperwork."

"Deal with it, princess. I could always put you in laundry with the witches. I'm *not* putting you in the mailroom because I know you want it. I don't trust you."

"Says the man hunting me," I grumbled. "You *and* the witches both want me dead."

Faust just grunted, but he didn't deny it.

"Start with the files by the window. Your commissary is in there somewhere."

I glared at him, but I got to work. I could be bribed with cookies.

I might not trust her yet, but I didn't want Rei hurt. She was just so small. I had a feeling she could handle herself, but still. I couldn't be in two places at once, and both Venus and Faust were after her. I could handle a powerless witch. I could handle a wolf too if I had my gargoyle, but these fucking cuffs had taken him away from me.

Speaking of that fucking witch, she came flouncing into our mailroom and started hitting on Dakarys and me. She wasn't my type, and she wasn't Dakarys's either. She would have been pretty if I didn't know so much about her already. She was all up in my face stroking my arm.

"I've never met a gargoyle before," she purred.

I caught her wrist before she could run her fingers over my scalp.

"Then perhaps you don't know that you shouldn't piss them off. What do you want, Venus?"

"Exactly. Why are you in our mailroom?" Dakarys said.

"I hear you can get things. Things they don't sell at the commissary."

Things we'd never get her no matter how much she hit on us or begged. We knew what she would use them for. She was already breaking Astrid's rules, and that didn't bode well for us.

"Why? What do you want?" Dakarys asked.

What the fuck was he doing? Everything we got for the witches went through a warlock named Darius. It was just how things went. Darius brought us a list when he picked up the mail, and we delivered it when we dropped off the mail. Witches didn't approach us directly. It was against the rules. It was Astrid's rules and our rules. It gave us less of a chance to get caught. Venus wouldn't have had a job yet, just like Rei, so she had free time on her hands. Did she not know Rei was with us, or did she think we were stupid?

Venus slid a piece of paper into his hands.

"Everything on this list."

Dakarys slid the list into this jumpsuit pocket and winked at her. He was up to something. He usually was.

"We'll see what we can do."

"Thanks! Maybe we can hang out. I'm bored."

I hoped she would go be bored somewhere else. This woman was vile.

"You can't be in here unless you are working. Maybe later," I said.

"Great. Bye, sexy."

Venus swayed her hips like she thought she was sexy as she left the mailroom. Like anyone could make our prison jumpsuits sexy. Venus certainly thought she could. As soon as the door closed, we went back to scanning packages. Dakarys hadn't even looked at the list.

"What are you playing at?"

"Witch games. Isn't it fun?"

"Not with our thief on the line."

The door opened again, and Darius slipped in. *Now* it made sense. Darius always brought the list from the witches nowadays. We were getting pretty good at figuring out what all the ingredients they asked us to get were meant for. We could even brew some poisons ourselves after chatting with Darius.

"What's the shit on this list for?" Dakarys said, shoving the list at Darius.

Darius looked over the list and frowned.

"A really nasty poison that not even Astrid will let us use. Who gave you this?"

"Your new witch is causing problems with our new friend Rei. We had an arrangement with Astrid."

Darius sighed.

"I don't like her. Astrid called a meeting, and we all agreed to leave Rei alone. Venus agreed too. What do I need to do to get these items?"

We weren't going to ask him to rat. We'd never do that. But this needed to be handled because Venus was out of control. She was defying the orders of her high priestess and asking us to help her kill Rei.

"You'd better get Astrid out of laundry and into the mailroom, Darius. We had this handled," I said.

"I'm Astrid's third. Are you sure you don't want me to handle this?"

Dakarys looked down at Darius's list.

"I know what these ingredients are for. Astrid wants a potion to bind a new witch to the coven. That can only be Venus. How would you handle this, Darius?"

Darius sagged.

"I have no idea. If I snapped her neck, I'd just make her a martyr. Several witches agreed with Astrid not to come at Rei, but they didn't want to. They thought your fox had anything Venus wanted to throw at her coming her way. Your fox is bringing a lot of drama into my coven."

I let out a little growl. This *was not* Rei's fault.

"Blame your witch for that. Astrid gave her an order, and she's the one that can't drop it."

"Your fox *bit* her."

"You've met Venus. Can you blame her?"

"No, I guess not. I don't like her either, and I don't particularly appreciate that she's disobeying Astrid. I'll get Astrid. She's not going to like this."

The witches had a monopoly on laundry duty. Astrid fought hard for that, and I had no doubt Venus would join them. They segregated us in our jobs. Since Dakarys and I were the only representations of our kind in Silverhold, they didn't put us with any of the gangs. There were plenty of us in prisons in other countries, I was sure. They didn't have anywhere to put us when we transferred. We lucked out with the mailroom. That's where they put people who didn't fit. I *really* hoped Venus didn't end up here with us because the witches shunned her.

Astrid burst into the mailroom and glared at us.

"We had an agreement! Your fox is safe, and we get our ingredients."

Dakarys shoved Venus's list at Astrid.

"Venus bypassed Darius and came to us to get her ingredients for poison. Which begs the question of how she knew to come straight to us and why she thought we would help her. You do realize our little business keeps going because we don't tell just everyone what we are doing. There are a lot of snitches in Silverhold."

"Venus must be watching me. She saw me meet with you before I called my coven about Rei. I don't trust her. That poison could very well be meant for me so she can take over my coven."

Well, shit. We *did not* need Venus taking over the witches here. The only reason we got along so well with them was because of Astrid.

"So, what are we going to do about this wayward witch?" I asked.

"*We* aren't going to do anything. Venus is my problem, and I'll handle it. I'll make sure she doesn't become your problem, though I'm still not sure why this fox is so important or why she's not with the other shifters."

I still didn't know that myself. We were risking so much protecting Rei and causing so much drama with the witches. And we still didn't know why Rei was hanging with us instead of her own kind.

should not have an inmate in here helping me with my paperwork. I was lucky the warden liked me because I had to spin about a million stories as to why I needed her in my office instead of fixing shit in mechanical with the other shifters.

It wasn't that I didn't want her around the other shifters so they could get curious about her too. She seemed to have pissed off a lot of witches. There was the one in here that wanted her, and I'd already gotten a message from the coven she stole the Grimoire from on my burner phone. They wanted her dead.

They offered enough money that I knew even if I didn't take the job, it was only a matter of time before someone else did. That particular coven was swimming in money. Enough to get an inmate out of Silverhold early and set them up nice and comfortable if they killed her and didn't get caught. Enough for someone to be willing to commit a crime and get caught to come here and complete the job for them.

I didn't know why. Even when I found out what she

was, I didn't want her dead. I should have. She was mouthy, and I didn't think she was the least bit sorry for all the shit she had stolen. She probably had every intention of going straight back to theft when she got out.

Still, I could respect that in a way. Stealing was her job just as much as killing people was mine. She had to be good at it if they could only tie her to one theft and being at the scene of another. There was nothing I hated more than sloppy criminals.

I had her in my office doing my paperwork because it was the only place I could watch her and keep her safe now that I knew they had put a hit out on her. Fuck. I was risking so much for this girl, and I didn't know why. She smelled better than anyone I'd ever met before. Why did she have to smell like that?

She smelled like diving into freshly laundered sheets under the full moon while someone was baking your favorite dessert nearby. It was like everything I liked at once, and now I had her right in the same room all day. I wasn't just curious about what she was. I was addicted to her scent.

And she was just so fucking adorable as she slammed my files around and called me an asshole under her breath. Why was this happening to me? I'd been on countless hunts. I'd never once sat there thinking about how cute my prey looked when they were frustrated. Maybe I should just take the job and kill her. I needed to focus.

I couldn't kill her without finding out what she was first. There were too many unanswered questions about her. I pulled my tablet out and connected it to my personal hotspot. I could settle this once and for all by finding her birth certificate. This hunt was getting too personal. I needed to stop focusing on her so much. If my mind weren't totally on the present, I would leave something behind and end up a resident in Silverhold.

I glanced up as she called me another name. She was getting pretty creative with them too. I let out a growl and focused back on my tablet. There was a record of every single supernatural birth, and she was of an age it would be digital. I typed her name in and…nothing. What the fuck? Supernatural hospitals were meticulous about this. Even if she were born in a human hospital, she wouldn't have been given a social security number unless her parents had updated this after the birth.

I still had her file on my desk. I hadn't given it to her to put it away. I looked at her social security number and ran it. She had a *human* social security number. I checked for a birth certificate again in human records. One didn't exist. The only record I was able to find for her was that she was adopted by humans and raised human.

She wasn't even remotely human. Did she even know what she was? The Fae had recently opened their gates, and not only started living on Earth, but they were allowing carefully vetted people into their realm. She wasn't Fae. I'd never heard of a Fae who could turn into a fox.

Was she from an entirely different realm? Why was she here getting raised by humans? I let out a little growl.

I couldn't kill her yet. I had to solve this mystery.

What did Faust do all day in this prison? It certainly wasn't paperwork. There were stacks all over this office. The fucker played on his tablet, sniffed me, and growled all day instead of helping me. I never did get to my commissary file, so I didn't even get my cookies. Faust was a dick.

He personally escorted me to the mess hall and leaned against one of the walls to let me eat. What did he think I was going to do in the mess hall? If Venus came at me again, I'd fight her with my fists like I did in the shower. I *was not* revealing I had the wrong cuffs on this soon. I might need my magic later, and I was only bringing it out if I had no choice. I was a lot of things, but I wasn't stupid. If only I could figure out how to get rid of Faust.

I met Dakarys and Rajack at the mess hall entrance, and I wasn't complaining that we got to skip in line because of their little side business. Dakarys bumped my shoulder.

"You're in for a treat. They have the peanut butter pie

tonight. It's the only decent food in here, and you can go nuts on the cheese tonight. They serve mac and cheese every night because it's easy and cheap. Grab the pie while you can and eat it first. There's never enough, and people will shank you for yours."

I had enough to worry about without someone stabbing me for pie. Even though it was neon orange, looked nasty, and made disgusting noises, my theory was right. It was impossible to fuck up mac and cheese. It could have used salt and pepper, but it wasn't bad. It was much better than the mystery meat. The gravy made it edible, but I'd always been more about the carbs than the protein.

I spooned double helpings of the mac and cheese on my plate and moved on to the pie, but Dakarys stopped me.

"With Venus and Faust after you, I'd take the meat too. We'll explain more when we sit down."

I just shrugged and dumped the meat and gravy on my plate. Dakarys and Rajack seemed to have their own table to themselves.

"So, the witch situation isn't handled. Venus either wants to poison you or Astrid. She came to us with a list to make it. That's not protocol for our business. Every group has a delegate that brings us a list for the entire gang. We get nothing unless it's on a list from the delegate and approved by their leader. Some things don't need to see the inside of this prison, and they know we won't get it. If it's dangerous, they'd better have a good fucking reason for asking for it."

Venus was a thief, but I didn't know if she had killed before. It wouldn't shock me after what she did to Hauser. The Vampires that went after him after she betrayed him could have killed him instead of just beating him three times. If she were willing to double-cross on a job, it wouldn't be too far off that she would try to kill Astrid to have every witch in this jail do her dirty work for her.

"So, what are we doing about Venus?"

"Nothing just yet. Astrid wants to handle it. She may eventually. I'd snap her neck if we didn't piss the witches off. We need them on our side."

"For this big plan you need a thief for? Am I going to find out what that is soon?"

"Soon. Trust building. Right now, we're just trying to protect you from Venus and Faust. We'll get there."

I was oddly okay with not knowing for now. I didn't just steal for anyone, and I needed all the help I could get in here. My gaze wandered over to the witch table. Venus was still sitting with them, closer to Astrid this time. She wasn't paying attention to the other witches. She met my eyes across the mess hall and made a slicing motion across her neck.

I'd never killed anyone before, but I'd make an exception for Venus in self-defense.

Faust was at the witch table in seconds. He glared at Venus.

"Are you making death threats, inmate?"

"Just saying hi to an old friend."

"I know all about your relationship to that particular inmate. Do you need to calm down in solitary? Because if you cause drama in my prison, I'll leave you in there until you go mad."

Faust's eyes flashed amber, and his canines elongated. Venus cowered back.

"We aren't going to have a problem."

Faust just created a massive problem for me. Right now, I just needed to worry about Venus. Venus and I were both kept in solitary until they moved us here. Probably for the exact same reasons for what was happening now. I nearly went nuts in there, but Venus looked rough when I saw her again.

Venus wouldn't come at me directly with the threat of solitary hanging over her head. She was a manipulative bitch. She was going to get herself some minions or take over the coven, and *they* were going to come at me.

Fucking Faust. He should have just stayed out of it.

DAKARYS

$\mathcal{A}$s far as I was concerned, let Venus rot in solitary. She was fucking up our plans in so many ways. We didn't just need a master thief. We needed Astrid to make a potion for us and ask as few questions as possible. We required the witches on our side. One witch was fucking up all our plans. She was trying to kill our thief, and she might try to take out our witch too.

Why weren't we killing her again?

I usually loved working in the mailroom, but I was a hot mess knowing Faust had Rei in his office doing paperwork. We didn't like it, and he had to have pulled a lot of strings to get an inmate as a personal assistant. Most inmates would have killed for that job if they weren't working for Faust. Most of the jobs here were menial and back-breaking, even the mailroom. Sitting down in an office would have been a dream if you weren't sitting in the same room as fucking Faust.

The only reason I wasn't totally flipping about her being in there was that Faust threatened Venus with solitary after she made that motion to Rei. He could have just wanted to kill her himself, but for now, he was protecting her. That gave us time to figure out our Faust problem. And having Rei in a COs office would work to our advantage. One of the things we needed her to steal was cuff keys.

I just hoped she opened up soon about the things she was hiding because we needed to hurry if we were going to get out of here. And at the rate she was attracting attention, we needed to get her out of here fast. Faust might protect her now, but we all knew he was a serial killer. He just had that vibe about him, and this was coming from an entire prison of deviants.

Astrid better be dealing with Venus if she wasn't killing her. The witches weren't due in the mailroom today, but we also told Astrid we weren't filling her list until they handled the Venus situation. Venus was a thief. If we gave the witches potion ingredients, she could easily steal something and make poison like she intended to do.

No one was due in the mailroom to make demands today. We were bringing in supplies today. There were cameras everywhere in prison, and we were supposed to scan all the packages. Rajack and I had an entire system for tricking the scanners and avoiding the cameras. There was a blind spot in a large corner where we could separate packages for delivery.

We should get loot for the Vampires today. They knew we couldn't get bagged blood, so most of their demands were pretty simple. The Vampires really liked kinky books and sex toys they were too embarrassed to ask their family to mail. They got pretty specific about their butt plugs and erotica with Rajack and me, but I guess asking your sister for that was some line that didn't need to be crossed.

Luckily, today's haul was all books, so we didn't have to worry about sex toys. There was some book series they were all into, and the latest book came out. One of these days, I would have to sit down and read the series because every single Vampire in Silverhold was waiting on these books.

Someone entered our mailroom when they weren't supposed to. No one was due today. Rajack and I both turned, and it was one of Astrid's witches. We knew this one well. She was in here on a murder rap and totally cutthroat. Astrid kept her in line but let her out to play if someone needed to go down.

"Hi, Wren. Unless this involves Rei, the witches aren't supposed to be in here today."

Wren tossed her white-blonde hair over her shoulder and glared at us.

"I don't give two shits about your fox. This is about the witch she pissed off. Astrid says you refuse to fill our order until she's dealt with. I'm here to tell you she has a plan."

"Are we going to be let in on it, or are we just being told it's handled again?" Rajack growled.

"Some people agree with Venus because they don't know the entire story. Some of our witches think we should take over the mailroom instead of laundry and corner your little black market since you won't get us shit if we hurt Rei. That's fucking stupid. None of us even know *how* you are doing any of this, and they are disrespecting Astrid by disagreeing with her."

Well, great. Ever since Venus got here, the witches wanted to kill our thief and plan to kill Astrid, and now they were planning to kill us. No one could blame this on Rei biting her. Venus was psycho.

"If Venus comes at us, we'll kill her and every witch with her," I said. "You haven't said how you plan to deal with this."

"Astrid doesn't suffer traitors, but we need to know how many there are before we deal with them. If we take care of business and leave anyone standing, we'll still be in this mess. I've buddied up with Venus. She thinks I'm her best friend in here. She's completely revolting. She got banned from her previous coven, and you have to do nasty shit for that to happen. Now, she thinks she can just walk in here and run things like every single gang doesn't respect Astrid in here. I'm not helping her recruit, but I'm taking note of everyone who agrees with her.

"Astrid wants to know if, when we have a list of names, you'll fill our order to deal with them."

Rajack and I didn't even need to talk about it. If Astrid was deploying a spy, Wren was going to be the best person for the job. Wren was a killer and could be a bit of a bitch sometimes, but I respected her after I got to know her. Astrid only authorized kills if someone hurt her witches, and she almost always used Wren to do the deed. Wren was a sneaky little bitch who could gut you in your cell and never get caught.

"We'll fill the order, but how do you plan to kill that many witches and not get caught?"

"Well, so far, only one has officially joined Venus. I'm just faking it. Venus is setting out feelers and whispering. I already know her plan. She wants to kill Astrid and blame your fox. She'll try to use the whole *I told you so* shit to insert herself as coven leader and send everyone after the fox. Once the fox is taken care of, she has her sights on the mailroom."

Astrid and Wren better hurry up because it sounded like Venus decided to upgrade from thief to killer and had a huge body count planned. Astrid better handle this, or Rajack and I would.

This witch wasn't just threatening my thief anymore. She's threatened my friends, my business, and me too.

REI

Faust must hate doing paperwork as much as I hated sitting here doing it for him. If no one could prove he was killing inmates, someone should have had a problem with these massive stacks of files. I still hadn't gotten to my commissary yet, and I'd been working on them for two days.

I hated him, but I was *bored,* and I talked when I was bored. I tried chatting with him. I hoped if I could fake liking him and let him get to know me, he'd drop this stupid hunt and let me work in the mailroom with my friends. Apparently, the psycho wolf wasn't very good at small talk. He grunted at me a few times, then told me to shut the fuck up. Asshole.

Faust escorted me back to the mess hall and then took a perch against the wall next to the witch table. I could easily find Venus in line because Faust was looking at her with murder in his eyes. It was pretty fucking rich. The wolf hunting me was looking to kill the witch who wanted to murder me so he could just kill me later. It was so fucked up.

Dakarys and Rajack met me at the back of the mess hall. They both slung an arm around my shoulders and led me to the front of the line. That was new. I didn't think they were touchy-feely. They were cool and quite lovely to me, but I thought that was just because they needed me alive to steal for them.

"I don't suppose we're getting more of that pie tonight?" I asked.

Dakarys just chuckled.

"Don't hold out hope for that one, Rei. There's no rhyme or reason when we get it. It doesn't come on the first of the month or the end of the month. It's random, and there's never enough. Be grateful they give us pudding on the days we don't get it. Apparently, before the pudding, it was this nasty lime Jell-O. Silverhold changed contractors for the kitchen, and now we have pudding."

I was bummed about the pie, but the pudding was decent, and I loathed lime Jell-O. They served it a lot in my elementary school. How fucked up that I got better desserts in prison than my school served me. Still, without the pie or peanut butter for lunch, I couldn't load up on mac and cheese, and it was those weirdly gray peas again.

"Grab your food in a hurry so we can get back to the table. Your friend Venus is causing problems with the witches. It's time to put our cards on the cable. Our cards and yours."

Oh, shit. Faust knew I wasn't a fox shifter because of his nose. Dakarys and Rajack probably had a million questions about why I had latched onto them instead of the other shifters. Everyone seemed to stick to their own kind in here. Dakarys, Rajack, and I were the only ones of our kind in this entire prison, but I was the only one pretending to be something I wasn't.

They needed a thief for something, but I really needed them more than they needed me. They could find another thief, but I couldn't exactly run to anyone else to help watch my back with the witches and Faust. This was Hauser's rule, and I'd never broken it before. He told me to keep my heritage secret for a reason. Faust was already on to me, and Venus was trying to get the witches after me. Unless I wanted to draw a lot of attention in Silverhold, I'd *have* to be honest with the two people who needed me for now. After I spilled the beans, I just hoped I didn't have a gargoyle and a sphinx after me too. Because I seemed to be making a lot of enemies in Silverhold.

I joined Dakarys and Rajack at the table, but they spilled nothing about their plan or asked me anything right away.

"We don't just need a thief. We need a witch. We have a working relationship with Astrid, and we *like* her. Venus doesn't just want to kill you. She's planning to take Astrid out and take over the witch coven here. Not only will our plan not work with Venus in charge, but Venus also doesn't plan to stop with you and Astrid. She wants to kill us too so she can take over the mailroom and our side business," Rajack said.

"You probably should have just gone for her throat with those little fox teeth instead of her ankle. It would have saved the prison from having to deal with her shit," Dakarys said.

Shit. I knew Venus was awful, but I didn't realize she

was this bad. She had no problem betraying Hauser, but I got why she wanted to take me out. I could even understand Astrid for standing in her way, even if I thought she was a bitch for it. But Dakarys and Rajack? Was she going to kill both of them just to take over the mailroom? Venus knew how to steal and move stolen items, but she wouldn't know the first thing about doing what Dakarys and Rajack were doing as far as I knew. I was a thief too, and I don't even think I could pull it off.

"So, why is Venus sitting over there getting friendly with the witches?"

Venus was getting cozy with a mean looking witch with bleached hair that looked like she could cut a bitch. She was little and scrappy looking, but so was I. Hauser always said the littler they were, the meaner they were. She was taller than I was, but she looked like she had me beat in the spitefulness department. I *did not* want to face off against that witch. She probably fought dirty.

"Oh, the one she's whispering with is Astrid's spy. Don't fuck with Wren. She's fiercely loyal to Astrid. She's listening and taking names. Wren is finding out all the traitors, and then the witches will deal with them. But with Faust so interested in you and the witch drama, we have to step up our plans."

"I'm listening."

"Not here. There are too many ears in the mess hall. We'll have this conversation in the one place we know we have privacy. After you finish eating, we'll sneak to the mailroom before the last count and they lock us in our cells for the night. We won't have a lot of time because they don't want us out of our cells unless it's yard time or we are working."

I nodded. We'd have more time if we ate faster.

Dakarys and Rajack had many questions for me, but I had a lot for them. What was so crucial in Silverhold that someone else couldn't steal it?

And why were they risking drama with the witches and Faust to protect me?

99

*M*oment of truth. We had our plan. We had almost everything we needed except what needed to be stolen. We had our thief, and we could use Faust's interest in her to get what we needed to escape. But the fox was hiding something and there had to be a reason she was with us instead of the shifters. It was just prison culture. You kept to your own. It was the same in Scorchwood, aside from a few odd groups.

I really hoped she told us the truth and it wasn't horrible, because I liked her. I seriously saw her call fucking Faust an asshole right to his face. *No one* here did that because we weren't stupid. I got this feeling Rei didn't care that he knew she thought that.

Venus was causing all kinds of drama. I saw her in the mess hall after she tried to attack Rei in the shower. Rei didn't have a mark on her, but Venus's mouth was all busted up. Score one for the fox because she told us Faust didn't even try to step in and stop it.

We all gathered around the mailroom table and leaned in.

"Bottom line, Rei. We need a thief to help us do something that has never been done before. We can't bring you in until we know we can trust you. We know you are keeping something major from us. Why are you avoiding the shifters?" Rajack asked.

Rei just sighed and squared her shoulders.

"Are there cameras in here?"

"Yeah, but there's a blind spot in the corner. The cameras don't have sound. Why?"

"I'll just show you. Can I trust *you?* Hauser told me to keep this secret no matter what. It's pretty major I'm showing you this. Faust suspects. It's why he's so interested in me."

Rajack let out a little growl. He wouldn't trust her until she revealed this secret, but I knew he liked her too. We talked in the mailroom. We both desperately wanted her to be in on this. With all the people after her in Silverhold, we wanted her out of here before someone killed her. We liked her, and we didn't want her dead.

"This Hauser must have had a good reason for telling you that, Rei. We'll protect you."

She must have trusted us just a little, or whatever reason she was hiding from the shifters must have been major because she floated off to the corner and turned to us. We saw this shimmery red cloud envelop her skin, and then she sprouted fox ears and a big bushy tail. But I was still looking at her human face. She didn't even rip her jumpsuit like shifters always did.

What the fuck?

Did she already steal a cuff key? And shifters just *could not* half shift like that. Sometimes, their beast would take over, and their features would change. If they were well trained, they got control and stopped the shift.

If they didn't, they turned into an animal. They *never* sat there with ears, a tail, and a totally normal face.

Rajack and I both jumped back.

"I'm not a fox shifter, but I can turn into a fox. The lady who did my cuffs was lazy and didn't take my blood."

Well, we could use that, but *what the fuck was she?* No one turned into a fox unless they were a shifter. Rajack was staring at her like she was utterly fascinating.

"You only have one tail," he said. "You're clearly young and haven't gotten up to enough trouble if you haven't earned more. I read about your kind when I visited Japan. I've never actually met one before."

Rei put her ears and tail away and joined us at the table.

"I've gotten into *a lot* of trouble, but I can't seem to earn another tail."

"What the fuck is going on? Because I don't know the first thing about creatures who can half shift or get extra tails!" I exploded.

Rajack was grinning like a total fool.

"We've got ourselves a Kitsune, Dakarys. A trickster demon. She's *exactly* what we need to break out of here, and the fact that her cuffs aren't keyed right will play in our favor."

Well, shit. There was a demon back in Scorchwood, but he just disappeared one day with his entire gang. He was the only demon there. Half the prison thought they all disappeared like people tended to do sometimes, and the other half thought since Scorchwood was in Hell, Amduscias figured out how to break out and got his people the fuck out of there.

I didn't know what the fuck a Kitsune was, but I

knew about demons. It would be a tremendous boon to have one on our side, especially if her whole demon thing involved playing tricks.

Rei was eyeing both of us.

"You need me to steal something to break out of Silverhold? That's never been done before, and it sounds like fun."

Just then, the bell rang for us to report to our cells for count. We didn't get the chance to tell her our plan, but I was thanking my stars our thief thought breaking out of a magical maximum-security prison sounded like a grand old time.

could not stop grinning. The guard in my cell block was this really nasty warlock, but nowhere near as bad as Faust. Brody was a bully and liked to use his shock baton for no reason, but he didn't have a body count. I was standing outside my cell waiting to be counted, and I had this big, stupid smile on my face.

Brody passed by my cell with his clicker in one and his baton in the other. I drew his attention, and he stopped in front of my cell. I didn't give a shit about Brody. He'd shocked me more times than I could count. It was Faust you had to worry about in here.

"Something funny, inmate?" he demanded.

Brody liked to shock people, but I *loved* fucking with him. He was this weasley warlock, and I could have beaten his ass all across this prison, even with these handcuffs on that took away my gargoyle. Brody just got so uppity when you made fun of him, and he gave me the perfect opening, even if I wasn't grinning about Rei.

"Your fly is open, Brody. The witches here wouldn't touch that pencil dick with a ten-foot pole. Did you fuck one of the rat shifters? I'll bet you did."

I cracked up laughing as Brody lost it. He shocked me in the stomach and kicked me into my cell. I stumbled back and fell into my cot, laughing. Brody finished his count, and Dakarys joined me.

"You know Brody is one of those purists that doesn't believe races should mix, right? If you had just pointed out he left his fly down, he probably wouldn't have shocked you again."

"I know all about what Brody thinks. He was so pissed when he found Wren with that shifter. He threw her in solitary for slumming with a wolf, and not a damned thing happened to the wolf. Can we beat Brody on the way out? We owe him for Wren."

"Don't be stupid," Dakarys hissed. "Are we going to take out every shitty guard in here? Want to go toe to toe with Faust?"

I just laughed. *Nothing* could spoil my good mood now that I knew just how much we'd lucked out with Rei. I was curious how she ended up here since demons rarely hung out on Earth. They had always fascinated me. They were so secretive, and there was an entire realm of them. I didn't even know what the different kinds were.

Every culture on Earth wrote about different kinds of demons they feared. I loved reading about all of them when I was free, but I had no idea how much of that was real and how much was just silly superstition. There was a demon in Scorchwood. I tried to ask. I did. I wanted to know everything about Hell and what kind of demon he was. He told me to get the fuck out of his cell, or he'd show me. I knew how my gargoyle matched up against almost every supernatural species, but there was too much I didn't know about demons. I got right the fuck out of his cell and dropped it.

I read about what demons they had in Japan when I spent seven months there on a job. My job before I got arrested was importing and exporting for my family's company. I love that job. I traveled all over the world, making contacts and finding items.

It was just fucking luck I met Dakarys in Scorchwood, and we hit it off. It was kismet we got transferred here and assigned the mailroom where they stuck people who didn't have a gang. We wouldn't have been able to get our little business up and running with other people in there, but someone got released, and someone else got dead. It was probably fucking Faust, but we couldn't prove it.

"Rajack? What the fuck is a Kitsune, and why are you so fucking excited about it?"

"I learned about them when I visited Japan, but I didn't know if they were real or myth. They are supposed to be hyper-intelligent and clever. Depending on how it's written, even her name means clever. Think about it. We all know she stole way more than that Grimoire. They just couldn't prove it. We got blood tested for the cuffs because they had to, but we know they are lazy when they can get away with it. It doesn't just play in our favor they were lazy with her. This is fucking major, Dakarys."

And I was just ass crazy excited I'd met a demon that wasn't grumpy fucking Amduscias. Rei was at least nice to me. I was sure she didn't know the first thing about other demons if humans raised her, but still. My thief was a fucking demon, and I was just so excited about that.

I hoped I could keep her when we broke out.

FAUST

I hated this fucking prison with a passion. There were no windows anywhere, and there wasn't even fresh air in the yard they gave the prisoners. It was a giant dome that they projected holographs of clouds and a moon on it. I knew better than anyone the prisoners in Silverhold were horrible criminals, but there were shifters in there. If they were going to take their cuffs off one night a week and let them shift, they needed a proper moon.

I had every access to my magic and my wolf, and this place was just fucking depressing. It smelled like BO and sadness no matter where you went, and it wasn't like you could open a window anywhere to escape it.

I looked forward to my days off and tonight started my four nights off before I was on for another ten days. I never picked up extra shifts even if I was hunting a prisoner I was being paid to kill. I went to a shifter bar for drinks at the end of my shift and spent the next four days at my very isolated cabin running as my wolf and eating what I hunted. It cleared my head and allowed me to focus when I went back to that hellhole.

Except as soon as I left and made my way back to the bar, I wanted to go back. My mind was on that fucking inmate and her unreal scent. I didn't want to leave her alone in a prison full of criminals, even though I knew full fucking well she was one herself. I didn't want to be running as my wolf while that fucking witch was loose in prison, wanting her blood.

I really wished I had stepped in when she showed up in the showers and thrown her in solitary. I couldn't do a damned thing about that now because I thought it was a good idea to just watch for a minute to see if the not fox revealed something. The fucking witch hadn't given me a single bit of ammunition yet, but it was coming, and now I was fucking off. I should be at that prison.

What was this fucking inmate doing to me? Why did I care? I was getting smashed at my favorite bar and forgetting about her for a night.

I took my usual seat at the bar and ordered my favorite whiskey. A pack of wolves brewed it and was terrific. Call me a snob, but even if I was a lone wolf now, I tried to support other packs by only purchasing wolf made products when I could.

I'd knocked back four shots and was starting to feel them. I asked for another because I didn't want to feel a fucking thing right now, and it was like she was still in the room where I could smell her.

"Another!" I said, slamming my glass down.

"What's your deal tonight, Faust?" Raul said as he refilled my shot glass. "You usually have two, play a round of pool, and you leave. No one will play with you tonight if you never stop drinking and if you don't get that look off your face. What's bothering you?"

I was buzzed enough to talk to him tonight. Raul was a chatty bartender, but he usually knew better than to try that shit with me.

"You ever meet someone who smells too good to be true, and you can't get enough of it?"

Raul gave me this knowing look.

"They smell like everything you love all at once, even though it shouldn't make sense together? And you just want to be around them and protect them, even if you hardly know them, and it might not make a lick of sense?"

"Exactly! And I can't avoid her either. It's not an option where I work."

Raul just laughed.

"Why would you want to? That's your mate, you big, stupid wolf. The same thing happened to me when I met mine. You need to claim her, or it's going to drive you mad now that you've met her."

She *could not* be my mate. I didn't even know what she was other than she was definitely not a fox shifter. How was I supposed to claim her, anyway? She was in prison for the next seven years, and she hated me. She told me that several times while she was going through my files.

Fucking fate. I hadn't even been looking for a mate. I wasn't one of those wolves that made stupid sacrifices to the moon, hoping to find their mate. Some of them even went to witches for tarot readings and spells to try to locate them.

I did none of that nonsense. I was fine on my own. Having a mate tended to make people crazy. Case in point, how I was acting since I met this inmate. What I should have done was get blotto drunk and take a run in the wood until I figured out how to ignore this.

My wolf was scratching at the surface. Our fucking mate was in a magical maximum-security prison with a witch who wanted to kill her. She was pretty, and there were rapists there. I'd killed a few that weren't jobs because they didn't stop in prison.

I slammed my shot glass down. Fuck my days off. I couldn't kill her. No one could.

I would find out what she was, claim her, and kill every last witch that tried to hurt her.

I fully intended to keep my head down and serve my time. I had all these grand ideas of how to do that in solitary because there wasn't much else to do. If I had to rot in solitary that long because they didn't want Venus and I in the same prison, then who's grand idea was it to stick us together now? I knew Silverhold was supposed to be the strongest magical prison in our area, and I was sure other countries didn't want to deal with Venus either, but what the fuck?

And then there was fucking Faust. I had no doubt he would kill me when he was done with his stupid hunt. The only reason he was up Venus's ass and keeping me in his office was that he didn't want her to get there first.

Yeah, I definitely needed to get out of here.

And honestly? I'd never broken out of prison before. It sounded like massive amounts of fun, and no one had *ever* broken out of Silverhold before. The bell rang for count before I heard the big plan or precisely what I was stealing, but if they managed to get contraband into the prison having just learned about computers, I had no doubts they could do this. I hadn't even figured out how to check my damned email on the prison computer.

We needed to have a meeting about this, but the only place we could safely talk with so many people who would either rat us out or demand to come with us was the mailroom. And Faust grunted at me he would be off for the next few days, so he was sticking me there because I couldn't be in his office unsupervised. Score. I wasn't just finding out how we were getting out of here. I'd have four days away from him.

So, who the fuck was shaking me and growling at me when I was trying to ignore that blaring bell? I rolled over and looked at two amber eyes that weren't supposed to be here today.

"On your feet and out for count, inmate. I don't want to have to do this every morning. No one gives a shit about your beauty sleep. Solitary is a shitty place. Don't end up there because you missed count. I'm actually trying to help you. If another guard were doing count, they wouldn't have woken you. They wouldn't have even come in your cell. Their clicker would have come up short, they'd sound any alarm you'd probably ignore too, and you'd be dragged straight to solitary. Get up and stand at the front of your cell."

Well, shit. That was the most Faust had ever said to me, and he had this unfamiliar look in his eyes.

"Why are you here?" I demanded, throwing my itchy gray blanket off. "I thought you were off the next few days."

"I picked up some extra shifts. Don't make me repeat myself."

I did what he said because I didn't want a repeat of solitary. I already knew he didn't want me in there because he didn't work in solitary, and it would fuck up his hunt. He wasn't doing this to be nice to me, keeping me out of there.

We couldn't have any secret mail room visits now. After breakfast, we had to report straight to work, which meant more time with Faust. He took his usual position in the mess hall to glare at Venus. I grabbed my breakfast with Dakarys and Rajack. They noticed Faust as soon as they sat down.

"What the fuck is he doing here? It's his day off, and he *never* picks up extra shifts," Dakarys said.

This *could not* be about me. He couldn't want to find out what I was that bad that he took on extra work when he never did before. He wasn't even playing fifty questions with me in his office like he wanted to know that badly. Was this part of his fucked up game?

"He's too interested in Rei for me," Rajack said. "This is more than what she is. That fascinates me too. Faust doesn't strike me as being super deep. He's fucking crazy. If he wanted to know that badly, why doesn't he bring her back to medical for a blood test?"

"It's some fucked up game for him, but I haven't figured out how it's played yet. He maneuvered things, so I'm in his office, but he's not interrogating me. I was supposed to be in the mailroom until he got back. He's not onto this little plan of yours, is he?"

Dakarys shook his head.

"He can't be. We've told no one, and if he suspected, he would have tried to kill us. He doesn't even know about our little business, or he would have tried. We bring good shit in. Everyone knows better than to rat on that pipeline and keep the goods hidden."

Faust was at my table as soon as the bell rang for

people to report to work. I could feel his eyes boring holes in my back as we traveled down the yellowed halls and floors to his office. He unlocked the door and ushered me through.

I couldn't find any rhyme or reason to the stacks of files, and he hadn't chosen to enlighten me or help me. He walked over to a pile and pulled a folder out to hand it to me.

"This is your commissary file. Everything used to be done by paper check, but we have it by direct deposit now. Go through that and read me the routing and account number. I'll get it set up. The commissary here has decent things, but they don't have everything."

Was Faust being…nice to me? He hadn't seemed to give a shit about setting that up before. He'd been totally willing to let me go through every single file in here until I found it.

"I didn't think you gave a shit."

Faust winked at me. What the fuck?

"You've earned it. I hope whoever is funding it is generous."

"He is."

Faust crossed his arms and cocked an eyebrow at me.

"Boyfriend?" he growled like it mattered.

"Why? Do you plan on hunting him too if I had one?"

Faust let out this little grunt like he totally would.

"Just making conversation, inmate. I was rude to you before."

"Rude? You're fucking *hunting* me to find out I am. You grunted at me when I tried to make a conversation with you. I've been digging through your files for days, and you just *now* decide I deserve my commissary that you should have done as soon as they processed me?

What the fuck? My mentor was a wolf, but he didn't fuck with people's heads."

Faust perked right up.

"A wolf taught you? Who was it?"

"Someone who is kind and not a psycho like you!"

"I'm not hunting you anymore, Rei," he whispered.

I almost didn't hear him. Since when did he use my given name? He always just called me inmate or the number they assigned me in processing. Did he figure me out already?

"So, what? You've figured me out, and this is the part where you kill me?"

Faust stalked over to me and grabbed my shoulders. He was pretty fucking intense when he met my eyes.

"I'm *not* going to kill you. You have my word, and I swear on my wolf. I'm not letting anyone else kill you either. That witch is going to be a problem."

Well, that was fucking major. Hauser *never* swore on his wolf unless he meant it, and it had to be a significant oath for him to break that out. I was now sure of one thing. Faust wasn't going to kill me, and he would make damned sure Venus didn't either. He now knew my mentor was a wolf, and I would have totally understood the gravity of what he just promised me.

"I don't get it. Did you figure out what I am?"

Faust went back to his desk and plopped in his chair.

"I still don't have a fucking clue, and I'm dying to know. But you can tell me on your own time if you want. I'm not trying to fuck with you. Some things have come to light. I'll explain later. For now, let's get your commissary set up."

I still didn't trust Faust. Just because he promised not to kill me didn't mean he wasn't killing people in this prison. I didn't need a psycho wolf up my ass when we tried to break out of here. Still, maybe he could solve my Venus problem.

Faust held out his hand.

"Bring me your file. I'll get your commissary set up. It takes forty-eight hours for the transfer to process, and then you can buy what you need. Get some flip flops because there are all kinds of nasty bacteria in the shower. There's a microwave in the kitchen, and you can buy noodle cups if you hate the food here. There's junk food if that's your thing. You can eat it or trade it. You can also buy toiletries. Lock those in the cubby in your cell because they get stolen often. I don't need to tell you there are bad people here."

Why was he being so helpful today? What the fuck happened after it was lights out for the night, and he returned in the morning? Because Faust was being super helpful for someone who acted like that when we first met and had stacks of paperwork like he didn't give a shit about inmates here.

"What is the catch? Why are you suddenly being so helpful?"

"I'm not a bad person, Rei. I realize I fucked things up when I met you. I guess I just got wrapped up in smelling nothing like you before and turned it into a game. It was stupid. You were probably terrified of being in prison for the first time, and I made it worse. I'm sorry."

Oh, shit. Did big, bad Faust just apologize to me and make it a good one? My eyes traveled up his uniform to meet his. He looked sincere and like he desperately wanted me to accept it.

I still didn't trust him, but something told me Faust was deeper than Rajack gave him credit for.

DAKARYS

hy was Faust fucking things up for us? I didn't even know what this was. If Faust wanted to know what she was so bad, there was a doctor who could have drawn blood and told him. He was letting an inmate run loose with magic, and it was like he didn't even care if that could eventually crash down on his head and get him fired.

Why was Faust so interested? I could admit Rei was easily the prettiest inmate in here. I wanted to run my hands through that long, white hair, and I loved how her violet eyes were always sparkling with some kind of trouble. I loved that she was probably only helping us because breaking out of prison seemed fun to her.

Rajack was filling me in on everything he knew about Kitsunes. How fucking lucky did we get? The fact that they could only nail her for so little was making a lot of sense. He didn't know how much of what he read was true or not, but they were also supposed to be fiercely loyal, which we definitely needed.

We just needed to get her alone in the mailroom to

fill her in on the entire plan so she could get to stealing. One of the major things we needed her to steal was a set of cuff keys, but Rajack and I had already discussed this sorting mail. It was way too dangerous to steal them from Faust. If Faust's keys went missing, he wouldn't report it like he was supposed to. He'd torture inmates until he got the keys back.

We'd already picked our target for whose keys got stolen. Rajack and I both hated Brody. He was inept and cruel. He wouldn't report his keys missing either. He was a fuck up and would have assumed he misplaced them. Brody would search for the keys himself and explore every single option that didn't involve murdering inmates before he reported his keys were lost. And we'd be long gone before that happened.

It helped that the guards here were just as bad as us criminals.

"Hey, we got the panty order today. Do you think Rei wants some?" Rajack asked.

I had learned my gargoyle friend had a bit of a demon obsession, and now that we knew Rei was a Kitsune, he was always looking at her with stars in his eyes. She was beautiful, I could admit that, but we hardly knew her. I *wanted* to get to know her better, and I liked what I knew, but I didn't want Rajack running her off.

"Rajack, you *cannot* gift lacy panties to a girl we just met. Especially not when we need her. Do you want our thief running for the hills because you shoved a thong at her? Some lingerie they ask us to get is indecent."

"Fuck off, Dakarys. You know your mind went there when I brought it up."

He wasn't wrong.

I'll bet she'd look spectacular in a little purple

number that would make her violet eyes pop, but I couldn't think about that, nor would I ever bring it up. Rei had no problem telling Faust he was a dick to his face. She'd probably maul us, and it wasn't just that we needed her. I didn't want her mad at us.

Yeah, maybe I was a little obsessed with her too. She was just so spunky.

"I'm not going to shove them at her, but I'm going to ask if she wants some of this haul. I'm not being offensive, but every single woman in his prison hates the undergarments here. You know some men want the lacy thongs too."

That much was true. The shifters liked to bluster about how manly they were, and they were always picking fights, but some of them were our best customers for the lacy stuff. Rajack and I totally didn't understand that. If we liked women's underwear, we would have owned it instead of overcompensating and keeping it this big secret. But enough about that.

"Rajack, offer her *anything* but panties. Everyone likes chocolate. Get her the good shit they don't sell at the commissary."

"We don't have chocolate today. The chocolate doesn't come in for another week. We have a lot of panties today, and we got extra just in case. Why not give them to Rei instead of one of the kinky Vampires like we always do?"

"Because we already know the kinky Vampires are into them. Need I remind you we need Rei, and I'm pretty sure you are into her."

Rajack just scoffed.

"So are you, asshole. You're just trying to play it safe."

I threw up my hands.

"You should be too! We can't pull this off without her."

"Which is why we should get her nice things."

"You're going to do this no matter what, aren't you?"

"I'll keep it classy."

"You know there's pretty much no way to give a girl you aren't dating that didn't ask for it a lacy thong and still be classy, right?"

Rajack just winked at me.

"Unless you're in prison and the undergarments they give you are ugly and uncomfortable. Every single woman in Silverhold has spoken, Dakarys. There's not a single woman here that doesn't ask for this. She'd be more comfortable in what's in this package."

"Maybe, but I'll bet you anything you want she punches you in the face for asking."

"Fine. If I win, you have to deal with the Vampires until we get out of here."

"You're on. If I win, *you* have to deal with them."

Rajack held out his hand, and we bumped fists to seal the deal. I knew better than anyone how hot black market panties were in here.

Still, there were plenty of perverts in here with us. Rajack wasn't one, but I knew he was going to get punched in the face.

REI

Time flew by in Faust's office now that he was actually talking to me instead of just grunting at me. More than that, he was talking to me like an actual human being instead of an inmate under his care. He wasn't asking me questions like he was trying to find out what I was either. He knew I was raised with humans, and he wanted me to talk about how hard that was for me.

I found him easy to talk to, but it was fucking weird, and I still didn't trust him. What the fuck caused this dramatic change?

After we left the privacy of his office, his demeanor changed. He got scary again. He was a little sexy in his office when he was joking and smiling with me. I knew how fucked up that sounded, but he had a friendly smile when he deemed to crack one.

I met Dakarys and Rajack, and Faust took his usual spot glaring at Venus. No peanut butter pie again. They said not to get my hopes up, but it was still the best thing they served in the mess hall. I know Dakarys was all about the pudding, but Hauser made this banana pudding that was to die for. I couldn't eat the prison pudding without dreaming about Hauser's cooking.

"Something's changed," I whispered when we sat down. "Faust is being nice to me. He promised he wouldn't kill me and said no one else was allowed to either."

"That's the kind of fucked up games he likes to play," Dakarys said.

"No. He swore on his wolf. My mentor was one. Wolves don't make that oath unless it's serious, and they don't intend to break it."

"Faust isn't a normal wolf," Rajack pointed out.

"I believed him. How sure are you he's killing inmates?"

I believed it at first because Faust was acting like a psycho from the moment we met. He was different in his office. He still gave off some weird vibes, but if he left behind a body count here, wouldn't he be serving a sentence right along with us?

"No one has any proof, but everyone here is scared of him and said a lot more inmates ended up dead after he got hired. Every single guard here is awful. Some are incompetent, and some are corrupt. We know why people end up getting shanked in here. They made enemies, and the incompetent guards looked the other way. But sometimes, inmates die here that no one had a problem with. No one could explain it, and no one claimed credit. Those started after Faust got hired."

"But if all the guards here are bad, how do you know for sure it's him?"

Why was I even trying to defend him? I was never the kind of girl that a few smiles and brief kindness had me defending an asshole. If I was dating someone and they proved to be a dick, I noped right out of that relationship so fast. There was just something about Faust in his office today that made me think Faust was a lot deeper than anyone in here gave him credit for. I knew he was dangerous. I wasn't too fucked up enough about this not to realize that. Please don't ask me why I was trying to figure that wolf out or his significant mood changes.

"There's not much to do in prison except watch your surroundings and figure out how to break the rules. People watch Faust. He's good at his job. He's probably the only guard in here who isn't totally inept at it. He's also the only guard who won't look the other way about anything. He can't be bribed. Someone tested those waters and got sent to solitary. It's fucking weird. You don't sign up to be a guard here unless you're fucked in the head. No one can figure out exactly how fucked Faust is, and he makes everyone uncomfortable," Dakarys said.

I held up my hand.

"Wait, a minute. Everyone thinks Faust is a serial killer because he's good at his job?"

"Don't forget the dead bodies," Rajack said. "The other guards here are ignorant. They'd leave evidence. Trust me, if there were a revenge killing in here, it would set off this entire chain of events. A shifter would kill a Vampire, and then the Vampires would retaliate. It's the same for every gang in here. A lot of the unexplained deaths were people who kept their noses clean here. They were dangerous criminals, but they hadn't pissed anyone off. The only time someone dies here that didn't piss someone off is if you end up here for fucking around with kids, and whoever did it will brag about it."

"Yeah, but there are serial killers in here. One of them could easily be knocking off inmates instead of Faust."

They both just shrugged like I totally wasn't understanding this. I guess I didn't. Faust could be creepy. Sometimes, he had this look in his eyes where I totally could peg him for being a prison serial killer. There was just something about his smile that told me there was a different side to this story.

"Whoever is doing it has access to the entire prison. You know, like a guard? Enough about Faust. You can't trust him. Let's get our trays put away and sneak off to the mailroom."

Yes, enough about the wolf. I was going to give myself a migraine trying to figure out his mood swings. It was time to figure out exactly what I needed to steal for us to break out of here.

We gathered around a table in the mailroom, and I waited to hear what this big plan was.

"Okay, Rei. If you think this is too dangerous, tell us now. We need you to steal a guard's keys, but it can't be Faust. We already have a guard picked who won't report we have stolen their keys while we get the fuck out of here. His name is Brody, and he's a warlock. If you're already out, let us know."

I shrugged. I hadn't picked a pocket for a good long time. I stuck to grand larceny, but Hauser improved my skills on that since he caught me trying to lift his wallet. Evil warlocks were easy targets. They usually carried a lot of cash and thought they were too powerful for people to dare steal from them.

"I'm in. What time frame are we on? The only guard I ever see is Faust. I've never met him. I'm going to have to come up with a plan. Faust doesn't let me out of his sight when I'm by the offices. I'll have to pick his pocket. How can we cause mass hysteria and get him in the same room as me?"

Dakarys and Rajack grinned at each other.

"Mess hall riot," they both said at the same time.

"Is that it? You just need me to pick a warlock's pocket? What else does your plan involve?"

Getting keys was a start, but we couldn't exactly walk out of this prison. Even if we got those cuffs off, we couldn't fight our way out either. The guards outnumbered us. They had shock batons and guns. I'd steal from a guard all fucking day if they had a plan that didn't involve me getting killed.

They both just grinned at me.

"The guard's offices are new. There is an entire wing of Silverhold that used to house their offices. Brody brought a hot plate in and started this huge fire. Oddly, he didn't get fired. He just got suspended without pay for a few weeks. They moved the guard's offices and put a steel door on the entrance. That particular wing leads straight out the prison, and no one goes in there," Dakarys said.

"We're going to have Astrid make a potion that will dissolve the steel door. She's already told us it's possible with the right ingredients. We sneak out, and we'll have to arrange a car to get us far away. That shouldn't be a problem."

"I might be able to help with that," I said.

Would Hauser help us? He did everything he could to make sure I didn't rot in here, and he tried to talk me out of stealing that amulet. I knew he could see the beauty in breaking out of Silverhold, but he was also super against ever getting caught. He'd managed that so far, and he taught me exactly how not to go down. If I had listened, I wouldn't be here planning how to break out.

"How do you plan on getting to this door without getting caught? They don't exactly give us a lot of free time. The bell is going to ring for last count any minute now."

"Yard time," Dakarys said. "Most of the guards are in the yard when a group goes out, and we do get free time then. We know where everyone goes then and can account for them. They are nowhere near that door. We just need to get there quietly, and that's totally possible."

I had many more questions, but the bell started ringing to get back to our cells for count. I was totally on board with this if I could get more details that I wouldn't die breaking out of Silverhold.

And I actually needed to lay eyes on my mark first.

I was so fucking bad at this. I *did not* date. If I needed to scratch an itch, I went home with a female wolf from the bar with the understanding it would be one night. I didn't do repeats. If someone asked, I got the fuck out of their bed. I never invited anyone back to my place because my home was sacred, and I didn't want crazy people knowing where I lived.

I asked Rei for her commissary file, not just to get it set up for her. She said her mentor was a wolf. I jotted his number down when she wasn't looking, and now, I was sitting here like a fucking idiot trying to get up the courage to call and introduce myself.

How fucking awkward would that conversation be? Hello, I'm your ward's CO, and she just happens to be my mate. How can I fix shit with her so she doesn't hate me? Shit, how could I even explain all this without having *him* after me?

Still, my alpha wasn't totally shit when he raised me. He taught me how to romance and date. It just didn't go hand in hand with killing people, and I wasn't really interested in anyone in my pack before I left. This was stupid. I needed to get over it. I picked up my cell phone and punched in this wolf's number.

"Who the fuck is this?" he demanded.

"Is this Hauser Lennix?"

"It depends on who the fuck this is and how you got this number."

"Faust Vensolv. I'm a guard at Silverhold."

"Rei had better be fucking okay, and this is not the phone number for the prison!"

"Rei is fine. She's locked in her cell for the night. They put her in here with the witch she was arrested with. The witch is going to be a problem, but I'm handling it."

"Then why are you calling me, and how did you get this number?"

I cleared my throat.

"I wrote your number down from her commissary paperwork. She mentioned her mentor was a wolf, and I was hoping that was you. We need to talk. Wolf to wolf."

"I know where you are going with this, and if you hurt her, I'll hunt you down and end you."

"That's not it. Not even close. I know she's not a fox shifter. They didn't give her a blood test in processing. I have no idea what she is, but I have no intention of hurting her. She's my mate."

The line went totally silent before he let out this little chuckle.

"No, shit? Since you know she's not a fox shifter, then I guess you know she's not feeling a damned thing you are, and you're going to have to earn it."

Well, that was progress. He didn't hang up in my face, call the warden, and get her transferred as far away from me as possible. I wasn't stupid. I wasn't about to have any type of physical relationship with her while she was in prison. It would be taking advantage as her CO. The power dynamic was off. We could do that when she got out and we were equals. And we would be. She would be my equal in everything, and I intended to spoil her rotten. I had seven years to fix this.

"Yeah, I get that, and I botched this up before I realized the truth."

"You'd better grovel, man. Rei can hold a grudge better than anyone I know. She's not totally unreasonable, but depending on how much you fucked up, you may need more than seven years to win her over."

"I may have made an ass of myself when I realized she wasn't a fox shifter like everyone thinks."

"Big mistake. I told her to keep that secret no matter what she did. They didn't figure that out during processing?"

"A lot of the staff here is lazy. We just took in another fox shifter a few days ago, so I'm guessing they just used the same spell on her cuffs."

"You're a guard there. Why didn't you bring her back and have it corrected?"

"I should have. I know that, but I wanted her to show me what she really was because I honestly still have no idea. The only reason I still haven't is because she's in danger. It's not just that witch Venus. The coven she stole from has a bounty on her head. I didn't take the job, but they were paying enough that someone eventually will."

I could only ever say something like that to another wolf who happened to be a criminal. He would understand it was a job, and it was nothing personal. He had to be good at what he did too if he wasn't here in Silverhold.

"Would you have taken the job if she wasn't your mate?"

"No. I only take jobs if people deserve it. Rei seems to have pissed off a lot of witches, but she doesn't deserve to die for stealing."

"Is Rei aware of the hit?"

"I haven't told her. She's got a lot on her plate getting used to prison, and that witch on the inside is up to something. I was hoping you could do something from the outside."

"Kill an entire coven? I'd do it for her, but that particular coven is huge and well connected. Rei planned to get into their estate for months. She normally doesn't leave a shred of proof behind, but that coven had many cats. They had a lot of double-sided tape everywhere to keep their pets from scratching. That's the only reason she left that hair behind. All their cats were black, so a silver hair raised a lot of questions."

Well, that answered a lot of questions, including how good a thief she was. It also raised a lot. Why was she caught in the parking lot of the museum biting a witch?

"What exactly happened at the museum?"

"Rei doesn't know her family. We know what she is, but we've only made educated guesses about what kind. She thought she was a fox shifter when we met too. It was hard for her to be raised by humans. She wanted that amulet to contact her ancestors and get some answers about herself. I tried to talk her out of it, but she had a plan. When Rei plans something, it's flawless. She could have stolen that amulet, and no one would have realized it until they saw the empty case. Rei saw Venus on the security cameras and improvised. Venus was the one that botched the theft and alerted the guards. Rei should have left instead of assaulting her in the parking lot, but she really wants those answers."

"We chatted about her human parents. She told me a little about how hard it was when she realized she wasn't like them. She had to keep it this big secret, and she was in a human high school too. She had no one to talk to about it."

"Yes, I know. Her parents kept secrets about her too. She asked them about her birth parents several times, and they refused to tell her. I've tried to help her by digging into her adoption, but they redacted most of it, and it was like she didn't exist. We both wanted the answers that amulet could have given. I didn't want her doing it, but she could have done it if Venus didn't show up. You can't trust that witch. I agreed to take a job with her because she begged me, and she double-crossed me. I nearly got caught, and I had a whole Vampire clan after my ass because I thought I was stealing the item for them."

See, that was why I worked alone. Killing people tended to be a solitary job unless they paid you to take out a sizeable group at once. I still didn't take on a partner then. I just got creative. My old pack would make group kills, but there was so much drama with that. If someone didn't pull their weight, everyone got fucked. And I wasn't shocked it was a witch who had caused so much trouble with Hauser and Rei. Most witches and warlocks were perfectly lovely, but when they went wrong, they went *evil*.

"Rei has pissed off a lot of witches. The witch gang in Silverhold isn't that bad. Their high priestess keeps them in line, but I've watched this Venus making friends. I can't throw her in solitary unless she does something. I'm thinking of making her dead if she keeps threatening my mate."

"I don't think anyone is going to weep if Venus dies. Venus has probably pissed off way more witches than Rei ever did. We're talking blood feuds with several covens. If she ever wanted to stop being a free agent and join a coven again, I don't know of a single one that would have her."

"The only reason I hadn't is that I didn't want any more attention on Rei. Everyone at the prison knows Rei and Venus are enemies. If Venus ended up dead, even if nothing tied back to Rei, people would still blame her. I need a plan before I take out the witch, so it doesn't come back on Rei."

"Good. And I don't think I need to tell you that you need to keep her away from the other shifters."

"I gave her a job doing my paperwork. She's with me during the day. I'm going to have to figure out something as to why she's not going to the yard with the other shifters when we unlock their cuffs and let them shift or use their magic for an hour."

"Listen to me, Faust. This is important. It's not just her scent. When Rei turns into her fox, it's not even remotely like a shifter change. She cannot go anywhere near that yard and be expected to change. Promise me."

"I'll take care of it."

"Good. Figure out the prison situation. Rei is like my

daughter, and I fiercely love her. You keep her alive for the next seven years, and you have my blessing to claim her if that's what she wants."

It was a start. Hauser was on my side, but now I needed to win over Rei. I still didn't have a fucking clue what my mate was. I didn't ask Hauser to tell me either.

I wanted her to trust me enough to tell me herself.

REI

I really needed to call Hauser, but it wasn't phone time, and my commissary hadn't processed just yet. But it would soon. I could just tell I could trust Dakarys and Rajack. I was sure they'd planned this down to a T, and they knew the prison way better than I did. But I always ran my plans by Hauser first. We had our own secret language that the prison wouldn't have any idea I was breaking out.

I was trying to ignore the morning bell again because it was hard sleeping in here. They did lights out super early like they expected us all to be morning people. Like we weren't all criminals, and that kind of activity was best kept to night. Seriously. I'd barely fallen asleep before the bell was ringing for me to get to breakfast.

"Look out! It's Venus with a shank!" someone growled in my ear.

I jumped out of my bed and threw my fists up. Venus wasn't even fucking there. It was just Faust again.

"What the fuck?"

He crossed his arms and smirked at me.

"You said you didn't like it when I shook you awake. You're awake now. Get to the front of your cell for count."

"Asshole," I grumbled, stomping out for count.

Faust made his rounds with his clicker. I guess I was glad Venus wasn't in my cell block. I could already guess she was making a shank or had someone in mind who she was sending after me. Faust turned on his heels at the end of the hall.

"Thirty minutes before breakfast. Some of you desperately need showers. That means you, Murphy. That's just awful. I can fucking taste it. If I don't see you head for the shower, I'm throwing you in solitary. Bring your clothes to the witches in laundry. I'm not your mother, and I'm tiring of telling you to wash your clothes."

Was I the only one who ever told Faust he was an asshole? I thought Faust was just being cruel until I got close to Murphy and got a whiff. He had dried food all over his clothes, and some of it was the peanut butter pie from a few days ago. And Faust wasn't lying. You could taste his stink. I would have stayed away from him even if he wasn't a fox shifter.

Except he got right up in my face as we walked to the shower.

"You too good for the other foxes, love?"

Maybe I was thanking that stink now. He wasn't using his nose to confirm I wasn't like him. I just needed to work a little magic. I clasped my hand behind my back and twirled my finger. I nudged his flip flops off his feet until he tripped.

"Better be careful," I called over my shoulder. "You wouldn't want to slip in the shower."

The other foxes must be nose blind because they helped him up. Not a single fox in my cell had tried to sniff out my secret. How curious. I stepped into the nasty shower and desperately wanted my commissary to buy some flip-flops for the shower. A girl took the showerhead next to me.

"We're all dying to know," she said, scrubbing her hair.

"Know what?"

"Why you're slumming it with a gargoyle and a sphinx instead of us. You aren't even on work duty with us."

Hauser prepared me for this. I could do this. He taught me everything he knew about fox shifters.

"Don't you think it's weird hanging out with an entire group of foxes that aren't your skulk?"

"It totally is, but what else can you do in prison? I'm Candra, by the way."

"Rei."

"Oh, we all know by now. You seriously pissed off the witches. I know the *real* reason you're all up with the gargoyle and the sphinx."

Oh, shit.

"Yeah?"

"They get yard time with the foxes since they can't put them anywhere else. I've seen them naked. To say it's fucking impressive is an understatement. I'd get me some of that too."

Oh, gods. Now I would never be able to look at them without wondering about what they looked like naked. I couldn't say I hadn't already thought about that when I couldn't sleep in my cell, but Candra just confirmed it.

"I haven't actually got any yet. How is that even possible in prison?"

Candra just laughed.

"Oh, it's totally possible. You can get away with a quickie during yard time if you hide behind the bushes. The witches have a makeshift temple inside the prison for their yard time. They will rent it to you for sexy time if you don't leave a mess, and you pay them. Pro-tip, they really like the candy in the commissary. It'll sweeten the pot if they are being bitchy about it. Maybe that could solve your little witch problem."

"With Venus? She's a spiteful bitch who blames me for being in here."

"Didn't you kind of bite her?"

"Everyone is so focused on the fact that I mauled her leg. If she were actually any good at stealing things, she wouldn't have had the guards chasing her in the parking lot, and neither of us would have gotten caught. Plus, I heard she left behind so much evidence at other crimes, they were able to nail her with more than just the museum theft. She would have eventually been caught, even if I hadn't bitten her."

Candra laughed.

"You really do regret nothing, do you?"

"I didn't intend to go down with her, but I got to the Museum of the Profane first, and that amulet was mine. I should have planned better, but I owed Venus for something else."

"I hope it was worth it because she asked me to shank you in the shower."

My head whipped to Candra so fast my neck popped. I took a defensive stance, and she just laughed.

"I told her no, stupid. I'm not about to stab you in the shower in front of every single fox in Silverhold. They'd kill me. None of the foxes will touch you, even if you won't hang with us. Whisper is our leader, and she knows Venus is asking. Don't be surprised if you see her with her face beaten in at breakfast. We get it. Foxes aren't pack animals, and none of us are family. Just try to say hi to us sometimes, and everything will be fine. We have your back, Rei."

Well, shit. I wanted to meet another fox for the longest time, then Hauser told me what I was. I'd been avoiding shifters since then, but the foxes were pretty fucking cool. I guess I'd committed a significant prison sin by not hanging with who everyone thought was my own kind, but the foxes were cool with that.

Not only did they *not* try to shank me in the shower, but it also sounded like Whisper put the beat down on Venus for asking. None of the foxes had tried to use their noses on me. If Venus was asking around for someone to take me out, I needed to make as many friends as possible. Hauser's guidance served me well, but this was prison, and I would have to break a rule.

"I'd like to meet Whisper and thank her personally."

"She'd like that. Whisper is in here for knocking over banks. She might want to trade tips. She's not mad you aren't hanging with us. I know it's a thing in here, but we know none of us is skulk. They put us together anyway, and we make do. We look out for each other. A fox isn't going to shank you, but another prisoner might, even if a lot of people here think that witch is way too big for her breeches considering she just fucking got here. Whisper! Get your ass over here."

A tall woman with bright red hair and green eyes

walked over wrapped in a towel. She gave me a friendly smile, then checked out my boobs.

"Nice tits. I was wondering when you were going to introduce yourself."

Did everyone here like my tits? Because Murphy was under the water, but he wasn't getting himself clean. He was staring right at them a jerking off, which I really didn't want to see right before I ate that nasty food at the mess hall. Whisper followed my line of sight and sighed.

"Murphy! What did I tell you about jerking it in the showers? Only in your cell! No one wants to see that. Get yourself clean and get out."

"Yes, ma'am," he grumped, grabbing the soap.

"What's his deal?" I whispered.

"Murphy? He caused some shit with an eagle shifter and nearly died. He's never been right since. He's never getting out of here either. I honestly don't think he gives a shit anymore. Faust gets mad when he gets dirty and won't shower. Murphy enjoys pissing him off in ways that don't set Faust into his serial killer ways. It's passive aggressive, and it's gross, but it pisses Faust off, so we deal with it.

"I heard you call Faust an asshole to his face, and you aren't dead yet. Call me curious. We'd protect you no matter what, but you have mad prison cred for mouthing off to Faust. *No one* does that here. We all have our little ways to annoy him, but never directly like that."

"I guess. Thanks for not shanking me in the shower. Do I want to know what you did to Venus?"

"She got gang piled by a bunch of foxes in the laundry room after everyone left. She's probably in medical now. She's not going to rat us out to the other witches because everyone here knows Astrid gave her an order to leave it.

Whatever her plan is, she can't make an enemy of her own kind in here. That's a death sentence here. Most everyone else isn't going to take her up on it if they ask because everyone likes Astrid. A Vampire might if she offers to become their donor, but only if they take a test sip and like it enough to piss off Astrid."

I nodded.

"Glad to hear a Vampire will kill me for tasty prison blood."

"The Vampires have it pretty shitty in here if they haven't found a donor. They don't even give them bagged human blood. They get stale pig's blood from a slaughterhouse, and I've been told it's chunky."

"Ew."

"Yeah, the Vampires here are desperate for donors, and many people take them up on it because their bite is erotic, and they are fiercely protective of people they feed on."

"Venus thinks Vampires are filthy bottom feeders and should all be exterminated."

Whisper just laughed.

"Get dressed if you want to eat. If the Vampires find that out, she's as good as dead. They hate racists. I take it you're sitting with Dakarys and Rajack again?"

"I like them."

"We've all seen them naked. We know *exactly* why you like them. Plus, they can get good shit. Can you tell them we are running low on that special tea, and we haven't gotten our panty order yet?"

I held up my hand.

"Hold up, you mean there's another option besides these panties that come up to my armpits and the bra that digs everywhere?"

Whisper just winked at me.

"Talk to your new friends, sugar tits. They'll hook you up."

I hadn't asked them for anything. The foxes had been kind to me and got Venus out of my hair for a little while. I could pass the message to my new friends.

And I wanted better panties.

RAJACK

*R*ei was late to breakfast, and Venus wasn't with the witches. In fact, none of the witches had come to the mess hall. Venus tried to take Rei on in the showers, and it worried us the entire coven had taken Astrid out and gone to her bathroom to hurt Rei. The only thing that was stopping us from hunting down every witch in this prison was that we knew Wren. Wren said she was handling things, and Astrid had a plan.

Rei had already complained about the early morning hours here, and the witches could be off dealing with Venus in their own damned bathroom. It didn't mean we weren't stressing. We were just about to find Rei when she showed up with a big smile and not a single mark on her.

I couldn't help it. I pulled her into an enormous hug. We were not at the huggy point of this relationship, but I couldn't help it. Dakarys and I swore to protect her, and it had now become way more than just needing her to get out of her. She was cool, and we liked her. It would have been miserable trying to work this out if she had been this awful bitch like Venus.

Rei wrapped her arms around my waist and hugged me back. She just felt so lovely there.

"What was that for?" she asked.

"You were late, and there's not a single witch in the mess hall. It worried us."

"They might be in medical with Venus," she said with a little shrug.

"Your doing?"

"She asked one of the foxes to stick a shank in my gut in the shower. They think I'm like them, and they thought it was rude to ask. They beat her in the laundry room."

"Score one for the foxes," Dakarys said.

"I have a message from Whisper and a request."

"Whisper gets bonus points for looking out for you. What does she want and what do you need?"

"Whisper says the foxes are running low on their tea, and they didn't get their panties. No one told me that was an option. Are there extra? Can I get some?"

"Ha!" I yelled, punching Dakarys in the arm. "I fucking *told* you. The Vampires are all yours."

"No way! This doesn't count. She totally would have hit you if you offered. Since she brought it up herself, the bet is null and void."

We sat down at our table, and I just grinned at her. I was in a good mood. I got to hug her, and I could give her something she wanted.

"Settle a bet for us, love. I was going to offer you some of our panty haul because it's a desirable item and everyone in here hates the prison-issued stuff. Dakarys thought it would offend you enough to hit me and want out of our little caper. The loser has to deal with the Vampires."

She threw back her head and started laughing. Gods, I loved listening to that. She had this musical laugh that just sounded like trouble.

"Before prison, I totally would have broken your nose. It's creepy to gift panties to coworkers. You'll get fired so fast, and your employer will end up with a lawsuit. Being in prison, it's different. What they give us is cruel and unusual punishment. They don't have anything small enough for me, so I swim in everything. The bra is technically too big, but it still pinches me everywhere and the underwear rides up my butt. How they pulled that off, I have no idea."

I was flat out beaming and wanted to gloat all up in Dakarys's face. See, I wasn't a savage. I didn't go around gifting panties to girls I'd just met before prison. Creepers and perverts did that. Prison was different. Gifting naughty panties in here earned you respect because they had to be smuggled in carefully.

"See? The bet is still on, and the Vampires are all yours."

"Fuck you, Rajack. It totally doesn't count. Whisper told her about the panties, and she's had time to think about this. If you just sprung it on her, she would have hit you."

"Um, hello? I'm sitting right here, and I can tell you exactly how I feel and how I would have reacted. As soon as the option for comfortable undergarments was presented to me, I jumped right on it. I wouldn't have hit Rajack. The bra pinches, and the underwear is constantly creeping up my ass. Do you have my size?"

The only reason I wanted to offer was because we totally did.

"We had an order for a Vampire who is about your size. She filed an appeal. She wasn't granted her freedom, but she got transferred to a minimum-security prison where they serve the Vampires human blood. We'll drop it off at your cell when we're dropping off the rest of them for the foxes."

Her smile totally lit up her face. Contraband panties always did that in prison.

Someone plopped down at our table. It was a pissed off Astrid and an equally angry Wren.

"I thought we had an understanding," Astrid hissed. "I told you I was handling Venus. Now, she's up in medical, and I've got a bunch of pissed off witches who weren't on her side before but want me to do something about it now!"

"I didn't touch her," Rei said. "She's been asking around the other gangs for someone to kill me for her. She asked one of the foxes to shank me in the shower. They took offense. I didn't know about it until they told me in the showers."

Astrid glared at Wren.

"How the fuck did you not know about this? You're supposed to be her shadow."

"You've seen her in the laundry room. She doesn't pull her weight, and she constantly takes bathroom breaks. I can't follow her on every single one without blowing my cover. Everyone should be on work duty then. She must be going to all the bathrooms she can and asking anyone she finds on a bathroom break. Honestly, I'm shocked this is the first time she's gotten jumped if that's her alternate plan. Why would you even ask a fox to kill another fox?"

"She did it on purpose," Rei said. "This is what she does. She knew she wasn't getting enough support from the other witches. She's been here long enough to see how things work. She knew Candra wouldn't have taken her up on it. She *wanted* the foxes to beat her up because she knew exactly what kind of support she would get from her coven. She's going to say I beat her up with the foxes, and she wants everyone upset with Astrid to get rid of her for Venus."

I'd met some pretty bad people in prison. Between Scorchwood and Silverhold, I'd met prolific serial killers and rapists. Most of them weren't the least bit sorry for what they did and could admit it was only a matter of time until they got caught. Most of them were totally psycho and would brag about their crimes to make themselves seem more powerful. Some were stupid enough to try to keep committing them while in prison, and they always got killed.

I'd met some stupid criminals and some evil criminals, but Venus took the cake. There were pecking orders in prison. Respect had to be earned. Everyone understood that. If you wanted to insert yourself as a leader, you challenged the one in place in front of everyone, so they knew who to give credit to when one of you ended up dead. Long live the king or queen.

These games Venus was playing was fucked up. You just didn't do that in prison, and it was going to bite her in the ass. If she had riled up the foxes because she wanted the witches turning on Astrid and coming after Rei, then she'd made an enemy of the foxes. If she was randomly going to bathrooms and trying to arrange a hit, she'd made even more. Every gang had someone or several people who did their killing for them. If you needed someone dead, you went to that person.

You just did not walk around prison asking random people to do your dirty work for you. Some gangs took offense at that like you were looking down your nose at them.

"I'm sorry, Astrid. I know you want to handle this your own way, but that witch is causing drama with more than just your coven now," Dakarys said.

I totally agreed. She got that beating from the foxes on purpose. She was already down. Someone should get into medical and just put a pillow over her face until she couldn't cause trouble anymore.

"Why couldn't you just let her have the amulet?" Astrid asked. "You're both causing too much drama."

I watched Rei fume.

"Excuse the fuck out of me? Venus didn't research the security of the Museum of the Profane. I *saw* her face on the security cameras I was trying to disable. She didn't bother finding out how to disable the alarm either. She just barged in and tried to use magic like the Museum of the Profane doesn't have wards for that. She would have gone down for that theft even if I hadn't bitten her."

"Maybe, but did you *have* to bite her? My witches are less offended that she got arrested and are more offended about the biting. Everyone in here knows if you're going to become a career criminal, you will eventually get caught. Venus is pissed she ended up here and blames you, but my coven gets it. They don't think you should have bitten her."

"If someone wronged one of your witch's mentors

and caused physical harm to them, would you let that slide or get a blow in when you could?"

"She's not wrong," Wren said. "It's just how things are. Rei said Venus got her mentor beaten several times. Rei has the right to take whatever revenge she wants for every single one of those beatings."

"There is no way to spin this without starting a war. If I say it was the foxes acting without Rei's orders, the coven will come after the foxes and Rei. I can't blame anyone else either. If my witches start coming after a particular gang for no reason, they'll know I condoned it, and they'll come for me personally."

This was so fucked up because it was true. Venus had clearly never been in prison before, and she hadn't bothered learning how things work before she started moving things in place. Even if Venus managed to take over the witches, she'd never keep that position. She'd pissed off *way* too many people here. And I didn't know what to tell Astrid because everyone here respected the pecking order and didn't play fucked up games when they wanted to take over.

How did we fix this shit without starting a prison war?

"I know how," Rei said.

Rei knew Venus better than any of us, and she was a fucking Kitsune. If anyone could circumvent a plotting witch and foil their plans, it was going to be a Kitsune.

"I'm listening," Astrid said. "I'll tell you if it'll work or not after I hear your proposal. You're just as new to prison as she is."

"You tell your witches several gang leaders came to you because Venus was approaching people about a hit. They were angry about it because it came from her instead of you, and witches rarely ask other gangs to handle their dirty business. I know I'm new, but I've been watching, listening, and learning how things work. You don't need to name who beat her. You just need to tell your witches Venus was breaking the rules trying to get an unauthorized hit done, and it could have been anyone. I've only met the two of you from your coven, but you seem reasonable. Won't that get everyone angry at Venus instead of starting a blood feud with another gang?"

"That would work right up until Venus got out of medical. If she intends on lying and naming you and the foxes, it's my word against hers. And a lot of my witches only agreed not to come after you because of Dakarys and Rajack."

"Did you tell them what she did to Hauser? Wren gets why I bit her."

"You have to tell them everything, Astrid. Now, while Venus can't whisper in their ears behind you," Wren said. "Tell them Venus and Rei knew each other way before the museum and what she did to her mentor. You know they'll think Venus had way more coming to her than a bite. It's time for me to tell them what she told me while I was working her. Since this is a tense situation, put her fate to a vote, but make sure to guide it, so it goes in your favor."

Astrid sighed. She looked more tired than I had ever seen her.

"I have *not* put anything into the universe to have this bad karma biting me in the ass. Who thought it was a good idea to put the two of you in the same prison, anyway?"

I'd been asking myself that as soon as I saw Venus. At

first, we were happy they both ended up here. We had decided against Venus, but if we met Rei and she wasn't cool, we would have approached her. We were stupid and selfish. We just wanted a thief so severely, we sat there rating their merits like they weren't real people with feelings.

We hadn't even considered what it was going to be like with both of them here, and it was biting us in the ass now. Rei seemed to think she was safe from Faust because he swore on his wolf, so we put him to the back of our minds as threats and were trying to concentrate on Venus.

Rei just shrugged.

"They kept us both in solitary before they transferred us like they didn't want us in gen pop together. I can't figure this out either unless they did it on purpose, hoping we would kill each other. They could only prove it was me for one theft, so I have a witch coven pissed at me, but a lot of people didn't like Venus before they proved she had stolen from several people."

Did someone do this on purpose? Rei had pissed off some witches. We couldn't deny that. Venus had pissed off several races, and I could see why someone would want her dead.

But who did they want dead by sticking them together? Rei or Venus?

REI

itch politics were so fucking complicated. I could probably sneak into medical and take out Venus. I'd never killed anyone before, but Venus was getting beyond annoying. I didn't understand why Astrid wasn't killing her either. Astrid and Wren said they'd call a meeting in the laundry room and discuss her fate.

I was on my way back to Faust's office. I guess he wasn't taking any of his days off. He turned to me as soon as the door was shut.

"That little witch that keeps threatening you was found in medical beaten pretty badly. Your handiwork?"

I scoffed.

"Like I'm going to cop to that and end up in solitary."

"I was going to tell you good job if it was. You should have killed her. She's going to come for you, eventually."

"You're pretty fucked up for a CO. Has anyone ever told you that?"

"Not to my face. You're the only one brave enough."

I looked over at him, and Faust had this weird

fucking look on his face. He had a soft smile like he liked me calling him a fucked up psycho, and his amber eyes were sparkling. I didn't know how to process that, so I didn't.

"I think you like it," I grumped, stomping over to his files.

"Rei, I wasn't going to tell you this, but I think you have a right to know."

Was he finally going to explain his massive mood swings? Because I was getting whiplash trying to figure them out.

"Okay."

"The coven you stole the Grimoire for put a hit out on you here. It's only a matter of time before someone takes them up on it. I'll protect you with my life, but you're in danger, Rei. It's not just the witches in here. It's an entire coven."

I wasn't shocked. It answered many questions as to why Venus was here with me all up in my face, and why the warden hadn't taken any precautions with the two of us.

"I'm not surprised. Someone stuck Venus and me in here together for a reason. No one has tried separating us. You sat there when she showed up to beat me up."

Faust cleared his throat.

"I would have stopped it if it looked like you couldn't handle it. Shit, Rei. I'm really sorry. I had the chance to throw her in solitary then, and I didn't take it. I can't do it now because she got a beating. I'm so fucking sorry."

He really did look like he was being honest. He looked like he desperately wanted me to forgive him. I still didn't trust him because this was some dramatic mood change, but at least he was being honest with me.

Faust could have very well been fucking with me, but I didn't think so. Ever since he swore on his wolf, I got the feeling everything he told me was the truth except for why he was acting this way.

"At least I got to punch her in the face."

"I have to ask, Rei. Do you want her dead? I can get into medical. It would make sense."

Was Faust asking my permission to kill Venus? Why would he even need that if he was a serial killer? I didn't like this kind of responsibility. It was one thing for me to talk about this with Astrid, Wren, Dakarys, and Rajack. It was entirely another for me to sic Faust on her. I didn't want that kind of power.

"The witches are supposed to be deciding her fate. Please don't step in. If Venus ends up dead, there's going to be a war in this prison. They'll be after the foxes and me."

Would he actually listen to me? This situation was going to implode any day now if the witches didn't handle this. The fact that there could be an assassin coming after me didn't surprise me, but I could really only deal with one person trying to kill me at a time.

"Of course. You're right. I can't be here all the time. I don't know what to do, Rei. I have to keep you safe, but I can't sleep here. The only reason I feel safe leaving you at night is that you're locked in your cell. They could pay a guard to do it, though. Fuck!"

"CO Faust?"

"Yes, Rei?"

"Why do you even give a shit if I die? Is someone paying you to keep me safe?"

Did Hauser know him and gave him a call to keep me safe? If he did, I hoped Hauser tore him a new asshole for hunting me. Faust stalked over to me and tucked my hair behind my ear. He looked at me so tenderly. What the fuck?

"No one is paying me, Rei."

"Then what is all this? Why are you suddenly being so nice to me?"

"I swear to you, I'll explain. Just not yet. I'll swear on my wolf if you want. It's just too early to tell you anything."

I spat in my palm and held my hand out.

"Blood oaths are nasty, and I won't ask you to swear on your wolf again. We can shake on it."

Faust's hand was warm and calloused in mine. That wasn't the most fucked up part. I *liked* his hand in mine. I felt this little jolt of electricity where our skin was touching. Our eyes met, and we didn't let go for a minute. What the fuck was happening? Because I certainly imagined that if his hand felt this good, I wanted to know what his lips felt like on mine. And I *could not* wish to kiss Faust.

I jerked my hand away and went back to the table with the files. Faust cleared his throat and went back to his desk. Neither of us spoke. I'd never had a spit swear to go this awkward before. Note to self—no more touching Faust.

Faust pulled his tablet out and started typing. I *really* wanted to send Hauser an email, but I wasn't going to ask Faust to borrow his tablet and ruin whatever the Hell this was.

"I'm doing some digging, Rei. The coven you stole from put a hit on you. They have a lot of money. I'm trying to figure out if they greased some palms to put you and Venus together. It's not unheard of. I've already tried speaking to the warden to get Venus away from you. She keeps saying there's nothing she can do about getting her out of here. I'm not saying she's as corrupt as the Warden of Scorchwood, but you don't get a job at a prison unless you have a reason."

Which was why everyone thought Faust was a serial killer. Why *was* he working here? It had to be miserable for him as a wolf. There wasn't a single window in the entire prison. Even his office was like a cage. Hauser didn't even like elevators because he felt too boxed in.

"Yeah, I get that part. From what I've heard, the staff belongs in here with the inmates. What's your reason? The entire prison is terrified of you."

"You aren't."

"Oh, I'm fully aware you could kill me and make my life difficult. Hauser didn't raise me to not go down without a fight. You changed the subject. Everyone here says you're the only guard who can't be bribed and is good at their job. They think you're a serial killer."

Faust just threw back his head and laughed.

"A bunch of criminals would think someone who does their job well is a serial killer. They don't have a single shred of proof."

I cocked an eyebrow at him.

"Are they going to get proof, eventually?"

Faust just winked at me.

"Even the great Silver Fox left a hair behind."

"Be straight with me, Faust. Are you killing inmates? How did you find out I had a hit on me? I would imagine if everyone knows you're good at your job and don't take bribes, the coven wouldn't have approached you to kill me?"

I *needed* to know because Faust was fucking up my

head. It terrified me when he was so gung-ho to find out what I was that he was making it this game. I was mostly just confused now. He was going out of his way to protect me, and there was this energy transfer the few times he touched me.

"I'm going to be honest with you, Rei. I'm keeping your secret and trying to protect you from other people getting curious. I hope you'll keep mine. I'm guessing your mentor taught you a code if he's a wolf. You don't steal everything you get asked to steal. There's a process behind what jobs you accept. Am I right?"

"Well, yeah. The coven who put the hit on me misused that Grimoire. I stole it and put it into safer hands."

"That's what I thought. I'm not here because I want to work in a prison. It's miserable in here. I have to wash the smell of body odor and sadness out of my hair when I get home. I'm sure you had a cover job to cover your misdeeds. This is mine, and I have a code just like you do."

I frowned. If he was a professional assassin, I could understand that. Hauser had one on speed dial, and he gave me her number just in case. In hindsight, Hauser probably should have given her a ring after Venus betrayed him for her instead of the Vampires who kept coming after her. If he was killing people as a job and he had a code about it, who was I to judge? I stole shit for money.

"But you're in a prison full of criminals. How do you pick who you kill?"

"How did you pick who you stole for? They have asked me about new inmates and I've turned the job down. I don't need to tell you our justice system is flawed. That coven you stole from put a lot of money into finding you and a lot of pressure on anyone who would listen. You'd be in here even if you weren't really the Silver Fox. They found a silver fox hair at the scene and caught a silver fox at the scene of the crime. Even if your hair didn't match, they would have fudged things, so it did. Some people in here had hits on them because people were angry with the wrong person. I dig into everyone. I can't figure you out, but I can smell a frame job a mile away."

"Figure me out? You know I did it, right?"

"Oh, you're guilty as fuck. We can both agree with that. I meant I dug into you when I was on the hunt. For the life of me, I have no idea what you are or where you came from. Someone went through *a lot* of trouble to keep you a secret. You must be someone special."

I'd never really thought of it that way. Every time Hauser and I hit a dead end, I always thought of it more that someone didn't want me and never wanted me to find them. Someone was trying very hard to avoid me and keep me out of Hell with the rest of the demons.

"Or I'm defective, and someone doesn't want me."

"No, Rei. That's not it at all. The only time I can't find a paper trail on someone is when they are important, and the government is involved. People try to cover their tracks all the time. I can always find that. The only time I've ever hit a dead end is when it comes from the top. The supernatural and human government worked together on your adoption to keep you hidden. You lived in the bum fuck Midwest for gods' sake. I'm betting you never ran into another supernatural until you moved away. Am I right? Let me guess. Your parents didn't want you to leave for college."

How the fuck was Faust reading me like an open book? The only other people who knew all this was Hauser. I grew up in a tiny town that didn't even have a movie theater or mall. You had to drive forty minutes to the next city for both, and my parents never wanted me to go. I thought they were just trying to ruin my life at the time, but was the entire point of that to keep the risk of meeting other supernaturals to a minimum? Why couldn't they just be honest with me?

"We got into this huge fight about me leaving for college. They only applied and would only pay for a college nearby. I was applying for scholarships and sending applications all over. It was pretty horrible. I was eighteen and wanted to see the world. I felt like they were trapping me, and they would never tell me anything about where I came from. I threw some things in their face, and they gave me an ultimatum. If I left, I was dead to them.

"I didn't think they were serious. They wouldn't speak to me while I was packing, and they wouldn't help me move. I called them when I got there to tell them I'd arrived safely and how excited I was. I've tried calling them numerous times since then. I've tried emailing too. I really am dead to them because they haven't spoken to me since."

"I don't know how to tell you this without upsetting you, Rei. I looked into them too. It's not that they are ignoring you. They disappeared around the time you must have left. Your mentor didn't find that?"

I sighed. Where the fuck were my parents? I told Hauser to leave it when he said he wanted to contact them because the fight before I left was so bad. I didn't look into them further either, outside of calling and emailing. Honestly, I didn't think they would have left their perfect house with the picket fence in a small town. I should have looked harder.

"I thought they hated me, so Hauser and I left them alone. I didn't call or email a lot. Just when I was missing them and to apologize for the fight. Fuck. I should have just flown back to check on them. You don't think they are dead, do you?"

"I don't know, Rei. There's no death certificate for either of them. You didn't exist until they adopted you, and they ceased to exist after you moved away. Even if I was a conspiracy theory nut that blamed everything on the deep state, this is some government level shit."

I shook my head. This made little sense, but pieces were starting to fall all around me that raised a million more questions than I already had. Fucking Venus. If she hadn't crashed my heist, I would have made off with the amulet and gotten some answers.

"If the government was involved in all this, wouldn't they have gotten me out of prison? If someone greased some palms to get Venus and me in here at the same time, why haven't they stepped in? I'm sure I was all over the fucking news if people in here know who I am."

"How do you know your people aren't working on it?"

Faust had been doing all this digging into my past, but he still didn't know what I was. He was being nice to me now and sharing theories. He hadn't asked me flat out what I was since he told me he was calling off his hunt and protecting me.

"Is this some ruse to find out what I am?"

"At this point, I'm just trying to keep you alive. I'm not going to ask you. If you feel comfortable telling me, it'll answer the million-dollar question. You tried to rob that museum for answers. I want to help you get them."

"Hold up. How do you know why I was at the museum?"

Faust cleared his throat. He'd better be very fucking clear on his answer because this entire conversation was leading to me being a member of Team Faust before he dropped that bomb.

"I called Hauser."

"What? Why?" I shrieked.

Faust was massive and could easily snap my neck, but I really wanted to smash his wolfy nuts with my knee and then break his nose. Did he call fucking Hauser because he thought they could be wolf buddies, and Hauser would rat me out?

"Calm down, Rei. Hauser was your mentor, and he needed to know about the hit. I hoped that we could take the entire coven out between the two of us, and I *never* work with anyone. There's no hit if the entire coven is dead."

What the fuck? Faust was willing to wipe out an entire coven to keep me safe. Especially *that* coven. Robbing the Aether Circle took a ton of planning, and none of my research prepared me for all those cats and double-sided tape. None of the cats in the house were shifters because that coven would have considered it slumming. If their estate hadn't been empty when I hit it, those cats wailing would have busted me, and they were constantly attacking me.

"You can't just wipe out the entire Aether Circle."

"Says you. I'm good at what I do."

"The Aether Circle is like a twelve headed snake. They are international and super connected. If you take out one chapter, the others will find out. They'll know it was professional if you got through all their security, and they'll launch their own investigation. They have *a lot* of money because they were using that Grimoire I stole to manipulate things. They will offer money for names, and you'll have them after you too. Don't invoke their wrath, Faust. You're seeing exactly what they are doing to me."

Faust just smirked at me.

"Well, princess. It sounds like you actually care if I live or die."

"I hardly know you, and I still think you are psycho, but you're kind of cool now that it's not directed at me."

"I'll take that for now."

Did Faust *want* me to like him? He was certainly trying hard. I mean, technically saying he would assassinate an entire coven because they put a hit out on me could be considered foreplay in certain circles. It definitely impressed me, even if I knew there was no way to pull that off without dying.

Now that he wasn't utterly terrifying, I could admit he was sexy in some weird, dark, murderous way. Hauser always told me that my attraction to bad boys was going to land me in jail.

He hadn't said anything about flirting with the bad boys when you were already in prison. He didn't have *any* rules for this. How fun.

SOTA

This had been going on long enough. I got why Rei had to be secreted out of Hell and placed topside, but I warned them several times about bringing her home as soon as possible. It wasn't just that our families had arranged for us to marry, and I'd never even met her. She'd pissed off a lot of witches, and now she was in prison. What did they think would happen, sending a Kitsune topside with no one to train her?

She should have had demons around her growing up. Even if they sent her topside and couldn't spare a Kitsune, she should have been sent with a demon guardian. They would have just cut that fucking witch's head off if Rei wanted that amulet so severely. The fact that she only bit her instead of killing her made it painfully clear she'd been away from Hell way too long.

Her father had permitted me to fetch her. Takahiro was the emperor of our portion of Hell, but we all still answered to Bael. All requests to go topside had to go through him. Technically, Hell was ruled by seven kings, but Bael was the most powerful. He agreed to let Rei go topside after she was born for her safety, but no one would give me an answer as to whose decision it was to send her alone. Probably because I was so angry about it, I probably would have hurt them.

We had every access to topside news and television in Hell. I knew it was her as soon as she got arrested. She looked exactly like her troublesome older brother. It was his fault they had to sneak her out of Hell in the first place. Only a Kitsune could cause that much trouble stealing things and pissing people off. She'd be celebrated in Hell for everything they slammed her for in the news, but topside was just so cranky about crime.

Hell didn't have a crime problem, but we understood certain demons were just prone to mischief. We taught them how to channel that. If Rei had stolen from witches in Hell, we would have only made her give it back and apologize. We didn't torture people here when things went missing. Topside was just so anal about theft.

I needed to get Rei out of that prison, and it was prime time she came home. I just couldn't do a thing until Bael permitted me, and right now, he wanted me to wait. I was going mad.

"I can handle this without Barbatos!"

Bael just chuckled.

"No, you can't. You're acting like a hothead, and he knows human and supernatural law. One of two things is happening here. They don't know she's a demon to send her here, and if that's the case, they have to be totally inept. The other situation is that they know and they don't care. Amduscias wasn't turned over to us when he got arrested. If that's the case, you're going to need someone who knows the old laws to get her out of there."

"Barbatos is off playing soldier in yet another realm. How long does he intend to be gone?"

"Oh, hush. He just met his daughter. If you can't kill people because your child wants to, how else are you supposed to bond? If they can pull this off, we'll have alliances with two new realms. You have tunnel vision about your bride. You can't go there without a plan."

"Have you talked to the witches down here? Because I have. They all say no one fucks with the Aether Circle and lives to tell the tale. Most of our witches haven't been topside for a long time, but they still know."

"You don't have to tell me about the Aether Circle, Sota. We kept track of all the covens who summoned demons. The Aether Circle was the worst, and if the demon lived to make it back home, they reported how awful they were. I can tell you exactly how big they are and how difficult it would be to take them out because we plotted several ways to wipe them off the face of the Earth for hurting demons."

I threw up my hands. I was way too old for tantrums, but if Bael knew how dangerous they were, why was he waiting for Barbatos to get back from playing in Olympus with his kid?

"If you know all that, why are we waiting for Barbatos?"

"Because even the Aether Circle is going to need time to get someone in Silverhold. She's safe there for now. Trust me. After the Scorchwood debacle, I know all about corruption in prisons. I know they can get to a guard. It only takes one, but they will have to ask around. There has to be at least one in there that will turn them down and move her to solitary for her safety."

"Kitsunes are not built for solitary. You know that, Bael."

"I'm aware, Sota. They need people to cause trouble with. It's where she needs to be since she pissed off the Aether Circle. We'll throw her an enormous party when she gets back that she was able to steal from them until she got caught."

"I want them dead. All of them. I know they can't summon us anymore, but they deserve to die for hurting demons and coming after Rei."

"We all want them dead, Sota. Believe me, we brainstormed several plans. Not even Solron could come up with something. She offered to hack them and steal all their money, but they'd just take it out on someone topside."

"I'm going to do it. I'm going to figure out how to kill them all."

"You're a Tengu, Sota. I'm sure once you get your bride back, a Tengu and a Kitsune can come up with a plan. Hell won't support you unless we know it will work."

My ancestors caused so much trouble on Earth before Hell decided to keep to itself. So did Kitsunes. Her father picked me as her husband for a reason. A Tengu and a Kitsune ruling that region would be quite the power couple. If her older brother hadn't been such a fucking problem, we'd be married already. Kudan was still an issue, but she could defend herself now, and we were getting close to pinpointing his location to take him out for good.

He was technically next in line, but he didn't want to wait his turn. He tried to assassinate his father and failed. His mother had been pregnant with Rei at the time. He managed to escape and had been hiding some-where in Hell. He had his minions hanging on his every word.

Everyone knew he would try again. Kudan knew damned well he wouldn't be allowed to rule after that. That didn't mean he wasn't going to try. Everyone knew he would have had no problems killing a baby, so that there were no other options for an emperor if he managed to kill his father. So, Rei got sent away for her protection, and I never got the chance to get to know her.

I was an advisor on the team that was set to hunt down Kudan. I should have been focused on finding him and taking him out. Rei couldn't come home until Kudan was dead. Except now she had to because some witches got butt hurt she took their Grimoire. The witches in Hell told me all about that book and said Rei did everyone a solid stealing it from them.

I felt totally helpless because I couldn't get permis-sion to get her out of prison, and I couldn't concentrate on finding Kudan. We'd zeroed in on a general location, and in four days, several legions in Hell would be storming it to see if we could capture him.

I couldn't help Rei until Barbatos was finished playing in other realms. I needed to focus on what I could do. I could get rid of Kudan and make Hell safe for her when I could get her out of prison.

This Brody I was supposed to steal keys from hadn't made an appearance in the mess hall until after I left Faust's office. He was glaring right at me too, like he blamed me for Venus ending up in medical. Okay, I was getting offended at all these witches, blaming me for shit and wanting to kill me. I owned stealing that Grimoire, and I'd do it again. Venus didn't disable the cameras at the museum. I saw her face clear as day. She wasn't wearing a mask. She'd be in here even if I didn't bite her. And I didn't lay a finger on her. She got her ass beat because she asked a fox to kill me. Why was I getting blamed for everything that went wrong with the witches?

It wasn't like I had this comprehensive plan to stop offending witches either. I was sizing Brody up for weaknesses to steal his keys. We'd hopefully be long gone before he realized someone stole them instead of losing them. He'd know I stole his keys, but good luck coming for me. I didn't know where we'd end up after we broke out. I didn't just need to hide from the authorities. The Aether Circle wanted me dead, and they would get personally butt hurt I broke out of here. It wasn't like I could stay in Silverhold either, even with Faust looking after me. He wouldn't be everywhere at once.

Brody was going to be an easy mark. I just had to make sure no one saw me. Brody was one of the evil warlocks. There were plenty of nice witches and warlocks if you didn't know that since they all wanted to kill me. Brody was not one of them. I could tell just by looking at those beady eyes of his.

He was shifty, but not in the paranoid way that would make stealing from him hard. He was one of those warlocks that thought his magic made him way too powerful to be a target. I hated those kinds of people. Honestly, I probably would have stolen from him just to prove a point in here if Dakarys and Rajack hadn't picked him for his keys. I would have done it just to mess with him, like stolen his phone so I could have one in here or his computer mouse to piss him off. I could be a passive-aggressive little kleptomaniac.

He even had douche bag hair. His hair belonged on some frat boy named Chad in 1998. I was glad they picked him. It would have been easier to steal from Faust, but I just couldn't do that. I didn't steal from people just because it was easy. Faust was honest with me when I asked if he was a serial killer, and he gave me an answer I could accept. There was a fine line between a serial killer and a paid assassin, and Faust had a code, so he didn't cross it. I would have said no and told them to pick another target if they wanted me to steal from Faust.

Brody kept glaring at me from across the mess hall and beating his shock baton against the palm of his hand.

I avoided meeting his eyes, even if I wanted to wink at him. I could use this. I already knew if Dakarys and Rajack started a riot, he'd make a beeline for me to give me a few shocks. I could use that opportunity to lift his keys. I'd take a few shocks for the team if it meant getting out of here.

I was starting to like Faust, but he was doing that overprotective thing wolves liked to do. It was entirely possible Faust would get to me before Brody did and ruin our entire riot so I couldn't get those keys. I liked that he looked out for me when it came to witchy killers, but not so much when it came to breaking out of prison.

I knew Dakarys and Rajack wanted out of here just as much as I did, but for different reasons. We couldn't put our plan in place without Astrid's help, and she was still dealing with Venus and her shit. The shit still hadn't been dealt with, and things looked tense at the witch table.

This seriously did not bode well for me. I had enough witches that wanted me dead without all of them in Silverhold siding with Venus. And it looked like several of them did, or the witches would have taken her out by now. Astrid and Wren wouldn't even be seen with us to give us an update. It was that tense over there.

It was this entire stalemate where I had three men offering to kill Venus for me, and we couldn't do a damned thing because witches were just so sensitive when you bit one of them. I could have used my magic and snapped her neck. Did they even think of that? I bit her instead of killing her because I had principles. Prison changed me. I'd already thought up several ways to kill her.

"Have any witches snuck into the mailroom with an update?"

Dakarys sighed.

"They haven't even brought us a new list. Wren was supposed to be stopping whispers of taking over the mailroom, but it sounds like it's spread. Astrid is doing her best with what she has. She and Wren are good at this. They'll put down the mini witch revolt and take care of Venus."

I liked Astrid, but I hardly knew her. Things looked pretty fucking dire at the witch table. I had this feeling showing weakness in prison was a bad idea, and now every single gang in Silverhold knew the witches were having problems. Perhaps they should focus less on killing me and taking over the mailroom and concentrating more on which gangs watched this go down and would swoop in for some revenge. I'd pissed off the witches. Surely, the witches pissed someone here off. I tended to do it more than other people, but pissing off people was a part of life, and none of these people would be in Silverhold if they didn't have the same habits as mine.

I really hoped this didn't reach blood feud level in Silverhold because I was pretty sure the Aether Circle had already declared one.

Astrid needed to handle her witches because if things got to blood feud level against me, then she was in danger too. So were Dakarys and Rajack.

I hated this. I hated watching the witches tear themselves apart because of Venus. Out of all the gangs in Silverhold, we had the best working relationship with them, and that was mostly because Astrid ran a tight ship. We were friendly with all of them. Some of them must have just looked at us as people who could get them shit instead of respecting what we pulled off with our black market because they were willing to listen to Venus about taking the mailroom over.

What they didn't know was that they could have it if they would just lay off Rei long enough for us to escape. We weren't going to leave Astrid high and dry, and we didn't intend to pay her for the potion we needed with things she couldn't get again. We would let her in on the big secret of running the black market out of the mailroom and let her take over.

There was this entire, long debate about taking her with us because we just really liked her, but it was too risky to break out with four of us. We felt rotten about leaving her behind, but we could set her up with a profitable business. Dakarys and I had a nice fund waiting for us when we got out to make sure we stayed hidden.

It was the Vampire's day to bring us their list of dirty books and sex toys. People needed what they needed to get through prison, and we didn't judge. Marcel always brought the list, and as far as Vampires went, he was the most tolerable out of everyone in Silverhold. He didn't always look at everyone like he wanted to eat them or fuck them. Or fuck them while eating them.

The only irritating thing about Marcel is that he didn't respect personal space. He got way too close to me and slipped me his list where the cameras wouldn't see it. He liked to sniff when he was close too, which was just creepy. Vampires did that a lot. They sniffed people way more than shifters did. Shifters could pull it off. It was how they got to know you, and they could sense your mood. It helped show them how to react around you. Vampires did it because you smelled like food to them.

I pressed my hand against Marcus's forehead and pushed him away from me.

"What did I tell you about that, Marcus?"

He ran his tongue across his fangs.

"I've just never sampled a gargoyle before, and you smell good. I'd make it feel good."

"You're getting pushy again, Marcus. Do you want what's on this list? Dakarys and I have already said we're off-limits for feeding, even if none of you have had a gargoyle or a sphinx before. We're proud, powerful supernatural creatures. We aren't finger sandwiches where you can try when you want."

Marcus just winked at me and flashed his fangs.

"Everyone is a finger sandwich to a Vampire. What's

going on with the witches? Are they plotting to over-throw Queen Astrid?"

We couldn't answer that. This could just be harmless gossip, and Vampires loved gossip, or Marcus could want to know this to bring it back to the Vampires. It wasn't just the Vampires either. Any of the gangs who had a problem with one of the witches but were backing off because of Astrid would be watching and waiting to swoop in. And some of them had issues with Astrid but hadn't taken her out because Wren would kill them. You had to be pretty fucking stupid to mess with Wren.

Wren was a pretty prolific assassin for her coven before she got caught. She was Astrid's assassin now. She might have those handcuffs on and no access to her magic. Wren might have been almost as small as Rei was, but she knew several ways to take people out anyway, and she was fiercely loyal to Astrid.

"Don't even think about it, Marcus. Wren will wipe out your entire clan if you even think about it, and we'll stop filling your orders. You'll never find out how *Blood Feud* ends before you die."

"We don't have a problem with the little witches, but some shifters do. There's a rumor going around it was the foxes that put that witch in medical, and you know the eagles and the witches are mortal enemies. Astrid and Tallon negotiated peace, but you know the only reason their people kept in line was because of their leaders."

All that happened before our transfer, so we didn't know all the specifics of why gang war broke out between the witches and the eagles. We just knew it was over. The witches and the eagles stayed away from each other, and Wren liked to brag about how many of them she'd taken out when they were fighting.

This was such a mess. The eagles had even bigger egos than the wolves, and they always bragged about how many countries put eagles on their flags. The list they gave us was pretty fucking pretentious too. Every gang had a hooch maker except the eagles. The eagles couldn't drink toilet wine like everyone else. The list they gave us involved imported bourbon and snacks from other countries. Most everyone here was happy with hooch and junk food the commissary didn't sell. The eagles didn't want food unless it was expensive, imported, and hard for us to get until we found a contact.

"Is it true your new fox friend is causing all the drama with the witches? She's cute," Marcus said.

"Stay away from her, Marcus. She's not food either."

We did not need the Vampires getting interested in her blood and wondering what she was. Faust was a little too interested in that. The foxes just accepted she was one of them, but we needed to get her out of here before more people figured out she wasn't a fox shifter.

Marcus wrinkled his nose.

"Not for *me*. Even though they act like they are superior to Vampires, shifter blood is just not good. I wouldn't mind bedding that one, though."

Fucking Vampires. If they didn't want to bite you, then they wanted to fuck you. Marcus had asked Dakarys and me for sex when we said he couldn't bite us.

"No fucking either, Marcus. Leave her alone."

"If the two of you are hitting that together, can I watch?"

"Get the fuck out of here, Marcus," Dakarys growled.

"At the rate you're pissing me off, I'm starting to feel like I don't want to get your shit."

Marcus held his hands up and backed away slowly.

"It's cool, man. We had prison counselors here for a little while, and mine said no question was a stupid question. I should always ask."

Marcus left the room, and Dakarys turned to me.

"I see why they fired the prison therapists if they told a fucking Vampire to ask every single question that popped into their heads. We need to keep them away from Rei."

"Astrid and Wren need to do something bold to corral the witches, or the eagles are going to swoop in and start another war. Not to mention the fact that they'll probably have the foxes as allies now."

"I feel so fucking helpless. We could try to sneak into medical and kill Venus, but it would just make things worse. If I had known she was going to cause a whole revolt and possibly start another prison war, I would have killed her on her first day," I said.

"I think several people in here wish they had shanked her before she caused so much trouble. It's too late now."

"It's fucked up people are still blaming Rei. Rei says she didn't even break in with a mask and was caught on camera. Venus would have ended up here even if Rei didn't shift and bite her."

"Yeah, but I don't think anyone else knows that, and no one is asking for the proper story. Everyone has heard Venus's side, and I'm sure she's telling it like she planned the perfect heist until Rei bit her."

"Yeah, but we don't want people approaching Rei and figuring out she's not a fox shifter. We can't start gossip either because we still need Astrid on our side."

Dakarys let out this huge sigh.

"You do realize this is going to get to a point where it's Rei or Venus, right? Astrid will be pissed, but Venus wants to kill her too. We can take credit, so they don't retaliate against Rei."

"Brilliant plan, Dakarys. Have you forgotten some witches are after us and our black market too? Let's not poke the witches. Astrid handled a gang war with the eagles. She can handle Venus and the witches."

I was less convinced. Astrid could handle her shit. I knew that from dealing with her. But she should have taken care of Venus by now.

This was going to end badly.

*H*auser seemed to think it was impossible to wipe out the Aether Circle, but I was digging deep to try to make it happen. I was deep in the rabbit hole of the Aether Circle. I'd dealt with corrupt covens for money. I saw criminal witches every day in Silverhold. The Aether Circle made them all look like girl scouts.

Supernaturals and humans put a lot of stock in the seven deadly sins, but for different reasons. For some reason, humans thought you ended up in Hell if you committed them while supernaturals knew that was an entirely different realm with demons who didn't like to visit Earth and kept a lot of secrets. No one took credit for the bombings of some greenhouses that apparently grew some witch ingredients for summoning demons. We couldn't ask them, but most people thought it was the demons.

The Aether Circle hit all seven pretty often. Rei had done the world a solid stealing that Grimoire from them. Try telling anyone that. The Aether Circle had people placed in politics, law enforcement, government agencies, and they threw their money around like candy to make sure of anything and everything.

I was a little fucking proud my mate stole from them and got away with it for so long. It was causing so much shit now, but I was going to keep her safe. She asked me not to, but I'd kill that witch in medical if she stepped out of line and tried to hurt her.

I'd already found the paper trail leading back to the Aether Circle. They had gotten to Venus. They paid for her lawyer and had already deposited a good sum into a bank account law enforcement didn't find, but I did. I'd traced a lot of money going in and out the Aether Circle. I also cracked the encrypted server they used for email.

Venus was supposed to kill Rei in Silverhold. The Aether Circle paid her and promised her she would only have to serve three years of her sentence once she did it. Venus was playing some sort of long game, and the Aether Circle wanted it done yesterday. That was why they reached out to me, even though they didn't know my name. They were putting feelers out everywhere.

Venus must have been pretty stupid if she thought they'd honor the deal if she didn't kill Rei. They wouldn't just not get her out of prison like they said. They'd pay whoever agreed to take the job on Rei to accept another assignment and kill Venus too. That was just their operandi. If you crossed them, you died. They didn't need the Grimoire Rei stole to make it happen either.

Taking them out would be complicated. Rei was right when he compared them to a hydra. They weren't even centralized in one location in the United States. They had a headquarters, which is where Rei stole their Grimoire, but not everyone lived there. There were plenty of coven members scattered throughout the States that would need to be taken out at the exact same time.

And that still wouldn't solve the problem. The Aether Circle was worldwide. They would all flock here, trying to figure out who arranged the hit. If I had the ability to take them out on my own, it would never be traced back to me. Bringing that many people in to wipe them out meant a greater chance of someone talking.

The Aether Circle had spells in the Grimoire Rei stole to get into someone's mind and make them talk. They could also control them for short periods. That was considered forbidden among the witches. Even Vampires were only supposed to use compulsion in extreme situations, mainly keeping their identity secret from humans. There were plenty of Vampires in Silver-hold for abusing compulsion and plenty of witches and warlocks for using dark magic. The Aether Circle had been getting a free pass for way too long.

Maybe I didn't need to kill them all. I didn't *need* to kill anyone. I was just good at it, and it paid well. I rid the world of a few scumbags. This called for a fresh approach. I was a rational wolf, even with so many people wanting my mate dead.

I wasn't going to kill them. I was utterly going to destroy this coven, sit back, and watch the fallout. Never fuck with a wolf's mate.

SOTA

*B*arbatos was still off playing in another realm with his daughter. There was nothing I could do about that right now. I was focusing on what I could do. Mainly, we needed to capture Rei's *kusoyaro* brother so I could bring her home safely when I got permission to get her out of prison.

Hell was a vast realm with many places to hide. It didn't matter what kind of demon you were, though. Patricide was frowned upon, and every region of Hell was looking for Kudan. He'd pissed a lot of people off, and everyone wanted dibs on torturing him. I'd been begging to get the honor, but it was really up to his father.

Takahiro had always spoiled Kudan. He gave the boy anything he wanted and made it go away when he got into trouble. Honestly, that was totally against the demon way of life. They should have tortured Kudan several times over for some things he'd done *before* he tried to kill Takahiro. I'll tell you this, if he had been properly tortured at least once in his life, none of this would be happening, and I'd actually know my bride.

The manhunt for Kudan had stepped up way before I made a stink about bringing Rei home. Kudan knew damned well everyone knew he was a *koshinuke* father killer and would revolt if he situated himself on the throne, but he was still trying. He sent one of his honorless minions to try to sneak into the palace and try again. He was quickly caught but killed himself before anyone could get information about Kudan's whereabouts.

Various demons had their own beliefs about what happened if you met the final death. This assassin wouldn't get the proper funeral rites we did if someone happened to die. We didn't know for sure because we couldn't ask anyone, but we believed his soul would never find rest, and he would have to walk the Earth as a restless spirit endlessly. Not all of Hell believed this, but we did.

There was only one place we didn't have eyes on to check for Kudan. Thanks to a deal with the Fae, there was a building for him to hide in, though technically, it was supposed to be having contractors in there, making it livable. Amduscias, one of Hell's dukes that had spent a lot of time in Scorchwood and broke out with the help of his wife, his husband, a Fae, and a wolf, gave us a tip about the prison. There were plenty of places Kudan could hide in there.

Amduscias was scheduled to visit Olympus with his mates, but before he left, he and all his prison buddies would come with us to Scorchwood to search for Kudan. All except his wife, who was quite pregnant at the moment. She wanted to come, and she was pretty effective with her fire magic, but everyone was making her stay home.

I was just waiting for them to get here. The familiar red cloud of a demon portal opened, and Amduscias stepped through with Roman and Skoll. I expected Fergus to be with Serafina, but I didn't complain that he came. He had fire just like Serafina did. I wanted Kudan tortured for centuries until he was begging for death before someone killed him, but I would have settled for watching Fergus use his fire dragon on him. I'd heard stories about how creative he was with making people die with it. I really just wanted Kudan dead.

I was leading this expedition, even if Amduscias outranked me in the entire Hell hierarchy. He was spat from the fires of Hell, so they gave him a title. I was a Tengu with parents, but we had mutual respect. Tengu were generally impressive demons, and everyone knew that.

"I'd like to take Kudan alive to be tortured, but I won't be upset if he's there, and we have to kill him. Kudan is not the fall on his own sword type. He has no honor. He'll use his minions as a shield because he's a *warugaki* and a coward. He thinks they *deserve* to die for him because he's owed the throne."

Fergus just crossed his arms and grinned at me.

"I know the type. We have them in the Fae realm too. Annoying little pissants who think they are owed everything and don't care what they do to get it. We've fought entire wars about it."

"If you wanted to get creative with that fire dragon of yours, I won't complain. I've heard stories."

Fergus just winked at me.

"It turns my wife on, and she likes to brag."

See, I wanted that with Rei. I wanted to learn all the fucked up things she did so I could brag about her all around Hell. Even though she was in danger from them, I wanted to shout from the rooftops she'd successfully stolen from the Aether Circle. Every single one of these men got this dreamy look on their faces when Fergus mentioned Serafina. I wanted that so badly, and I didn't even know what Rei's favorite food was because of Kudan.

"Is it true you can make his head explode?"

"If I shrink and fly into his ear. If I fly down his throat, I can do the entire body, but it's super messy."

I wouldn't have minded that, but Amduscias disagreed.

"Can we avoid exploding anyone? It took me ages to get burnt warlock out my hair when we were breaking out of Scorchwood."

Roman was a Vampire who always seemed to have this mad look in his eyes and frenetic energy. He kept fidgeting, and it was making me nervous.

"I like it when Fergus makes people go splody, but if you don't want a mess, I can rip his head off."

Wouldn't that technically cause a mess too? Vampires were so weird. We didn't have a lot of them in Hell and none in my region. They always stared at people like I stared at a plate of *takoyaki,* hot from our chef. They looked at you like you were their favorite food, and every Vampire here was attached to someone who let them feed on them. Roman was married to both Amduscias *and* Serafina, so he really shouldn't be looking at me like a plate of *gyozas.*

"It's so uncouth to try to kill your father, and it's a pretty big rule here never to hurt another demon unless they ask you to. We can't just kill Kudan, no matter how much he deserves it. Even his little minions need to be tortured for plotting to hurt another demon. It's the law. Did you want Serafina to plan how it happens when they finally decide to kill him? When she puts her head together with Solron and Charley, she plans beautiful executions. Did you know she planned Zepar and Warden Skinner's execution after the whole Scorchwood and takeover nonsense?"

He said it so proudly, and those stories reached us even in my region. Would Rei be good at that? I wanted to know every little thing about her. I couldn't do a damned thing until we took care of Kudan.

"I agree. Take him alive if at all possible, but if you can't, I think everyone in Hell would breathe a sigh of relief if he were dead."

Amduscias just shook his head.

"But they won't get the satisfaction of knowing he suffered a really long time first and begged for it. Male Kitsune are nowhere near as powerful as the females, and Kudan is soft. Between all of us, we can take him alive."

"We don't need him portalling out of the prison if he's there," Fergus said. "I've followed the Scorchwood renovations. They are working on the prison down below. I traveled all around the prison when I was digging into it. Warden Skinner never stayed there, but she had apartments near the guard's quarters. I would lay odds Kudan is in her old apartments, and his followers are in the guard's apartments."

"I agree. From what I know about Kudan, he wouldn't be caught dead in the shit hole that is the rest of the prison, even if everyone in Hell wants a few centuries with him in their dungeon," Amduscias said.

"Has Kudan met the Fae before?"

I shook my head.

"He's been in hiding well before you got here, and he's not old enough to have been around when the Fae were here negotiating Scorchwood."

"Good. Then he won't recognize a Fae portal. He'll know a demon one straight off and open his own to get out of there. Stand back. If he's holed up in the warden's apartment, we are about to catch him."

Thirty years of hunting him. Thirty years away from Rei. There was no other place he could be except Scorchwood. It was in a frozen wasteland area of Hell where no one lived.

He *had* to be there. And I was coming for him.

*A*s much as I hated my time in Faust's office before, it was kind of nice now that he was talking to me. He told me the Aether Circle paid Venus to kill me and bribed a few people to make sure we both ended up in Silverhold together. That wasn't super shocking, given what I knew about that coven, but Venus was even dumber than I thought if all she had tried to do so far was jump me in the shower without a weapon and get herself beaten up by the foxes.

If the Aether Circle paid you to do something, they expected results because if it was a job they didn't do themselves, they paid a lot of money, and there were perks offered. Venus should have been focused on just me instead of worrying about taking over the witch gang and mailroom. The Aether Circle would pay whoever took the job to kill me a little extra to take her out for failing. No witnesses, no one to spill their secrets.

"I got you something, but keep it a secret," Faust said.

I cocked an eyebrow at him. Why was he buying me things? Faust opened his desk drawer and handed me a pink box. I just stared at it. What game was Faust playing? He let out a little grunt and opened the box. This absolutely gorgeous strawberry cupcake was sitting in the box. I fucking *adored* cupcakes, and strawberry cake was my favorite, but why?

Faust reached into his pocket and produced a candle. He stuck it in the cupcake and lit it.

"Happy birthday, Rei. I know it's shitty celebrating it in prison. I got you this, and my gift to you is to let you make an unrecorded call from my cell to Hauser."

What the shit? I'd been so wrapped up in prison drama, and I'd forgotten my own birthday. My parents always made this big deal about it, but I didn't really celebrate that much after our fight. Hauser and I could never find out if the day we always celebrated was the day I was actually born or the day they adopted me. They really tried to make that day memorable for me, and it felt strange to do anything without them.

Hauser knew this and kept things low key. He'd make my favorite meal and give me a loaded gift card to my favorite bookstore. I could always be bribed with food and books. And, apparently, cupcakes and illegal prison phone calls, because there was this weird fucking feeling in my gut that Faust would do this for me.

"Hauser ratted you out strawberry was your favorite. I got it from this shifter bakery that makes my favorite cookies."

I eyed Faust. He was solid, cut, and didn't have a single ounce of fat on him. Even I could admit he was fucking hot as shit.

"You don't look like you partake of cookies, Faust. You look like someone who doesn't eat carbs, drinks kale, and gets up at some ungodly hour to run ten miles and lift weights."

Faust broke into this huge grin, and I realized I liked it when he smiled at me.

"I'm a wolf, Rei. I can eat all the carbs I want, and I *love* sweets. I wouldn't be caught dead drinking kale, though I like it as a side dish with steak. The only time I run ten miles is late at night when I shift and run as my wolf. It's my time to think and be me. I don't have a gym membership or a home gym. I look like this from being in the woods as my wolf."

Should I say it? Would it make things weird? Shit was already odd if he brought me cupcakes, and I never had a problem shooting my mouth off and making things super awkward.

"You should keep doing that because you look amazing."

I immediately blushed and shoved the cupcake in my mouth so I didn't have to say anything else. Since when did I get embarrassed sexually objectifying someone to their face? Faust just threw back his head and laughed. I embarrassed myself even more because I finally got a taste of that cupcake. He said shifters made it and there had to be some sort of shifter sex magic baked into this cupcake. It was fluffy, light, and just the right amounts of strawberry to buttercream.

Faust let out a little growl, and his eyes flashed gold when I let out a huge moan. Was he getting turned on watching me enjoy this delicious birthday cupcake? He set his phone on the desk and turned his back to me.

"I'm going to make a show of locking you in and pretending to go to the shitter. I'll try to make it last as long as I can, but I can't be gone long."

I caught his hand, and I felt those sparks again that I felt every time he touched me. I should have let go, but I liked it. I squeezed his hand.

"Thank you. This means a lot to me."

I still didn't know *why* he had done this for me, and maybe he would eventually tell me. But big, bad Faust, who the entire prison was afraid of, was a bit of a cookie-eating softie, and I dug it. I knew he killed people for money. I was sure the Aether Circle offered him a *lot* to kill me in here. He didn't take the job. He brought me cupcakes and offered me his phone to call Hauser instead. Maybe I'd eventually figure him out.

Faust shut the door, and I heard the lock click. I dialed Hauser's number. Faust and Hauser must have been talking often. Why, though?

"Is this Faust or Rei?" he demanded when he picked up.

"Hi, you mangy old wolf! I miss you!"

"Rei, thank the gods. Ever since Faust called me out the blue, I've been worried sick."

"You seem to talk to my CO a lot."

"You're lucky he called me instead of taking the job, Rei. He has his reasons. You stick to him like white on rice. You can trust him."

I could feel that I could trust Faust in my gut, even if I didn't entirely know why he was doing all this. If Hauser also said I could trust him, then Faust would be my new best friend in here. Still, I had a plan, and I couldn't stay here. I needed to be somewhere the Aether Circle couldn't find me. I couldn't risk anyone overhearing, and I didn't know if Faust's office was bugged. I used our code. We worked this out so we could talk in public or on non-burner phones and still discuss business.

"What do you think about Belize when I get out?"

Belize was our code for running from the po-po or being in a shit situation and needing an extraction. We didn't exactly have any code language for breaking out of a maximum-security prison, but he would understand.

"I think Belize is going to be fucking impossible, Rei."

"What if I had help and a plan? I would just need a ride to the airport."

"I'd give you a ride, Rei, but you should forget about Belize. Going there after prison is going to be impossible. The consequences for breaking parole are pretty severe. You'd be in prison a lot longer."

"What if the plan is good?"

"I still wouldn't risk it."

"I need to be where the Aether Circle can't find me. Venus is playing some long game. She's trying to take over the witch gang here. It won't just be one. It'll be all of them."

"I should have taken care of Venus when she betrayed me. Faust has a plan. It's insane, and it's just in the first stages of conception, but you might not have to worry about the Aether Circle when he's done."

"Just a gang of witches being led by Venus."

"Faust will take care of them. Trust me."

"*Why* is Faust all up in my business? I'm not complaining, and he ended up being cool once he dropped the whole psycho thing, but what does he get out of this?"

"It's not my place to say. He'll tell you when he thinks you're ready. I like him, Rei. I like that he's in there looking after you where I can't. You need a wolf in your life."

"I've buddied up with a gargoyle and a sphinx too."

"No, shit? I've never met either, but sphinx are supposed to be very tricky, and gargoyles make excellent protectors. Good job picking your prison gang."

"We were *all* planning to make a trip to Belize."

"Their idea or yours?"

"Theirs, but they know Belize better than I do."

"Does Faust know?"

"Fuck no."

"You should bring him in on your little trip to Belize."

Why would Faust help me break out of Silverhold? I knew Hauser liked him and trusted him, but he wasn't always right. I was about to ask why he thought my fucking CO would be on board with me breaking out of here, but I heard the key in the lock. Faust was back. I couldn't talk about this in front of him, no matter what Hauser said.

"I have to go. Faust is back."

"I mean it, Rei. If you ever want to make it to Belize, Faust is your best bet."

"I'll take that advice into account. Bye, Hauser. I should be getting my phone time set up soon. I'll call again."

Faust settled down into his desk and smiled at me softly. He just had this look on his face like if I asked him to help me get out of here, he'd do it.

But I'd been wrong before about men, and while he might help me out of here, I was pretty sure that didn't extend to Dakarys and Rajack. I liked them too, and I wasn't leaving them behind.

SOTA

This had to work. Amduscias was leaving with his family to run off to Olympus with Barbatos, and no one else in Hell was as familiar with Scorchwood as them. I couldn't search every nook and cranny of this prison without them. Not without tipping Kudan off and having him find a new hiding place.

I stepped through the Fae portal, but I wasn't in some apartment staring at Kudan. I was in a hallway. What game was this Fae playing? We needed the element of surprise! He would portal away if we kicked the door down.

Fergus placed his finger over his lips and shooed us back. I'd never seen him do this, but everyone in Hell was aware he could turn himself into a fire dragon. I watched him disappear entirely, and a small dragon made of flame appeared before me. Then, it just disappeared. I moved towards the door. I didn't know what kind of games they played in the Fae realm, but this was serious.

Amduscias grabbed me and pulled me back.

"He's shrunk himself to an ember and flown through the lock. He's seeing if Kudan is inside. It's the best way. Kudan won't know he's in there."

Well, wasn't that really fucking effective? Fergus wasn't in there long. He came out, dragging Kudan with his hands in flame handcuffs and another around his neck.

"Any sudden movements, and I'll burn your head off. Think it's hot now? Try me."

Kudan met my eyes and gave me a cruel smile.

"Sota. You won't take me."

Fergus twisted his arm.

"We have already taken you."

A kindly looking older woman appeared in the hallway and stretched her hand out to Fergus.

"Oh, please! Let my grandson go. He means no harm."

I transformed into my sacred bird and pecked her eyes out. That was no harmless woman. There was a mouth on the top of her head. She was a *Yamauba*, and we didn't need her here. If she knew we were here, then his other minions did too.

Roman licked the blood spatter from his face and frowned.

"She tastes bad."

Skoll popped him on the back of the head.

"What have we told you about eating blood spatter? It's gross, Roman."

We didn't have time to talk about Roman's eating habits. Yokai started spilling into the hallway with knives. Fuck. They weren't mighty compared to a Tengu, but they were tricky. I called to my sacred bird as Skoll shredded his clothing and turned into a wolf. Amduscias took up half the hallway as his black unicorn. Roman was bouncing around, ripping heads off.

Everyone was focusing on getting to Kudan. Fergus dragged him into the apartment and kicked the door shut. I could hear crashing in there as we battled the Yokai, who followed Kudan. He had a few foxes with him, and they had surrounded Skoll. Most of Kudan's followers were *Obake*, meaning they could turn into animals, but you should never call them a simple shifter. It was more complicated than that.

Roman was eating all the big cats around him, and the sight was brutal. He was covered in blood and getting it on everyone else. Every single Yokai tried to stay away from Amduscias. They were *toroi* if they followed Kudan, but they weren't dumb enough to try to take on a massive demonic unicorn.

I spread my wings and swooped towards the foxes. I had a huge, sharp beak and deadly talons when I was my celestial bird. I jumped into the fray and started mauling everyone I could that wasn't Skoll. Eyeballs and throats squelched and erupted under my deadly gifts.

I let out a shriek when the last body fell and shifted back. We all did. The crew renovating Scorchwood was going to have a huge mess to deal with. There was blood everywhere. The warden's old apartment was deathly silent.

Skoll scowled and raked his bloody fingers through his hair.

"I forgot how miserable this place is."

The heat was on in this prison area, so it wasn't horribly cold, but it was still dire in here, even without the dead bodies. I threw the door open to the apartment. Fergus was sitting up and rubbing his head.

Kudan was gone. He portalled out. We lost him.

This was a wonderful birthday, even if I was in prison. Faust didn't make me work on his files, and he didn't just bring me that delicious cupcake. He brought leftovers with him for lunch, and it was this fantastic goat cheese pizza. He cooked it himself too. I didn't take Faust for a pizza-eating, cupcake delivering wolf, but I was here for it.

I was leaning back in my chair, patting a massive puppy belly.

"What else do you do besides cook amazing pizza? Tell me something no one else knows about you."

"I will if you will. And it doesn't have to be what you are either. Tell me a secret, Rei."

"You have yourself a deal."

"I live in a cabin in the woods. I own ten acres of land, and I built my house with my own two hands. I love being out there, and I've never brought anyone home. I've been fine with that, but I'll be honest. It's starting to feel a little lonely."

He looked at me with his amber eyes like he wanted

me to be the first person who saw the cabin he made. And that was way too much pressure. I was a serial dater with commitment issues, and Faust looked vulnerable right now. I always fucked things up and ran before they could hurt me first. And I *never* dated shifters because they could scent I wasn't what I said I was. I avoided the supernatural community in general and stuck to humans when it came to dating. I shouldn't even be thinking like this about Faust. Or Dakarys and Rajack for that matter. Jobs were jobs. Feelings shouldn't get involved.

"Why hasn't anyone seen your place before?"

Faust just smirked at me, and gods, he looked so sexy when he did that.

"That's not how this game works, Rei. It's your turn. You can ask me something else once you've spilled a secret. And that's how it goes. This game is a lot more fun with beer, but I can't sneak that in here."

I let out a groan.

"Please don't mention alcohol. I could really go for a cold beer or warm sake."

Faust laughed.

"I'm sure you can get hooch in your cell block. We haven't tossed the cells or bathrooms in a while. Every gang does something different with theirs. You're stalling."

"No, I just perked up when you mentioned booze. There's a difference. You already know a lot about my past. I'm trying to think of something you couldn't find online. I'm assuming you've already dug through my social media?"

"Does that upset you?"

"Are you still stalking me?"

"No. I'm stalking the Aether Circle now. I'm going to bring that entire coven down."

I usually would have noped right out of there if anyone had dug through my adoption records and social media and admitted it to my face. I should have been doing that with Faust instead of sitting here sharing secrets and eating his pizza and cupcakes. So, why wasn't I? Why was I so drawn to him? Maybe because he was willing to wipe out the entire Aether Circle for me. As far as impressive things guys could do for girls went, that was right up at the top.

"Okay, here's something you might not have found. How did you know pizza was one of my top foods outside of Hauser's steak and mac and cheese? Did he tell you?"

His entire face just lit up.

"He didn't, and I didn't know. It's one of my favorite foods too. You've had Hauser's steak, but you haven't had mine."

That feeling was back in my gut. I mean, Faust was offering me his meat. It came from a cow, but I was seriously wondering about *his* meat. What the fuck was happening? It was time. Hauser said I could trust him, and I already told Dakarys and Rajack my secret. Nothing terrible happened, and they were trying to help me keep it. Faust needed to know. Yeah, I guess I did trust him too.

"Faust, I want you to know that—"

I was cut off. An alarm started blaring throughout the entire prison, and someone started screaming in Faust's walkie.

"Code Red! We're on lockdown. Get everyone to their cells!"

Faust immediately snapped to attention.

"Shit, Rei. Hold that thought and stay close to me. Silverhold is going to be locked down for a while, and your cell is going to get tossed. Don't panic. If you have anything in there, hide it!"

What the fuck was going on? I stayed close to his back as we walked down the hallway to my cellblock.

"What's a Code Red?" I hissed.

"They found an inmate dead. I won't know more until later."

Shit. Dakarys and Rajack better be okay. Did Astrid finally take care of Venus? I wouldn't be mad about that. Sitting in my bunk waiting for news was going to be miserable, but at least the foxes were friendly with me, and I'd have someone to talk to. I hoped it wasn't someone I knew.

The foxes all looked relieved as soon as I set foot in my cellblock. Candra flung her arms around my neck and squeezed me.

"I'm so glad it wasn't you."

Faust banged his shock baton against the wall.

"No touching, inmates. Stand for count," he growled.

He was back to being scary again, but I got it. Someone had died, and he was doing his job. We all scurried off and stood in front of our cell doors. Faust didn't even look at me as he walked down the cells with his clicker. It said a lot about Faust that everyone was dying to know who it was, but no one said a fucking thing.

He got to the end and turned on his heels. He grabbed the walkie on his shoulder.

"Cellblock D is all accounted for."

Guards started chiming in. No one was missing. A

few more guards stormed into my cellblock and started tossing shit everywhere. I didn't have a lot of stuff in my cell, but my thin mattress and shitty pillow were now on the floor.

There had to be some serious hiding places here because they didn't find a single shiv or any of Dakarys and Rajack's black market items aside from hooch. I was seriously going to have to ask where to stash shit because they could not find me with Brody's keys after I lifted them. And I wanted some black market shit too.

After our cells were a total cluster fuck, they locked us in and wouldn't turn the lights out. Were they seriously not going to feed us? I didn't know the protocols for prison murders, but I should probably find that out. I just stuffed my face with Faust's delicious homemade pizza and that cupcake, but I was a stress eater. And a bored eater. This qualified as both.

"So, I'm going crazy, and this is my first prison murder. I was working in Faust's office the entire time. Does anyone know who it was or if anyone claimed it?"

Wait, a minute. Technically, I *was* with Faust the entire time except when he slipped away to let me make a phone call. Did Faust do all this for my birthday because he needed ten minutes to kill someone? No. Faust wouldn't do that. I was getting to know him, and he wouldn't play me like that, would he?

"We thought it was you or that witch. Most of the prison feuds have been settled except yours. We didn't do it," a fox called. "Faust could have struck again."

"Faust was in his office with me. It wasn't Faust. Do you think the witches took care of Venus?"

"I doubt it. Sneaking into medical is hard. You have to be injured to get in. They will let you visit, but you have to be fingerprinted in and out. Killing someone in medical is stupid. You'd get caught," Whisper said. "Astrid doesn't use poison often. She usually sends Wren. Wren always makes it look like an accident, so it can't be tied back to the witches. I get what went down with you and Venus, but I'd avoid pissing off Astrid or Wren. Wren isn't dumb enough to make it public she's coming for you by asking around. You won't know until two minutes before you die."

"Couldn't she technically sneak into medical and kill Venus if she's that good?"

Candra laughed.

"It's not her style. Too many risks."

"Are they going to feed us or turn the lights out?"

Every single fox in my cellblock started laughing, and foxes tended to sound weird when they did that.

"It depends on who it was and how it was done. If they were smart and make it look like an accident, that's how they will rule it. If they stuck a shank in them, we aren't getting out of here until they've pinned it on someone, which means finding a weapon. Usually, any weapon. They will bring us shitty sandwiches and an apple, keep us locked in, never turn off the lights, and keep tossing our cells until they find something so they can pin this on someone.

"They don't get super deep into prison politics. They round up everyone stupid enough not to hide their weapons well enough and bring them down to solitary. They interrogate them until they start mixing up their stories because they are going crazy in isolation. Eventually, they pin it on someone, and they never come out of solitary. If they found you with a weapon, they'll let you back in gen pop once they've decided you've suffered enough, and they got extra time added to your sentence," Whisper said.

They bolted my bed to the wall, but I had just managed to get my thin mattress back on it. I tossed my pillow on the bed and flopped on my back. I was bored, and a bored Kitsune was going to get into trouble. I couldn't just lie there and talk with all this going on.

Who died, and who did it? This was like reading a book I had been waiting for ages for, finishing it in one night, and only having it end in this massive cliffhanger. Then the next book wasn't out for an entire year. This was way worse than that. I didn't even have other books to keep me occupied. I was going to go crazy in this tiny cell. I needed something to do.

I didn't intend to be here long, but I wanted to be comfortable. And I needed a weapon. I wasn't about to end up in solitary the next time someone died in here. I needed to find a hiding place. I'd barely started searching my cell when I heard a baton against metal.

"Out for count!" Faust yelled.

Why was Faust counting again? No one in here was missing. He didn't just count us this time. He shoved everyone into their cells and frisked them. When he got to me, he pressed me up against the wall and ran his hands over my body. I *should not* be getting turned on by this.

"Heads up, Rei. Someone stabbed Astrid in the laundry room. It had to because of Venus. They will come for you next," he hissed.

Oh, shit. The one person between every witch and me in here trying to kill me had just been murdered. I *liked* Astrid. It wasn't that she kept her people in line and was vital to our plan to get out of here. I didn't think she liked *me*, but I thought she was pretty cool.

"I'll protect you, Rei," Faust growled.

And I knew that. I knew Faust would take out every single witch in this prison if it meant keeping me safe. That protection didn't extend to Dakarys and Rajack, and I needed them safe too. I was getting attached.

I was so fucked.

AFTERWORD

Remember the Museum of the Profane where the infamous ankle biting went down? It's part of a new shared world. There will be a library, a museum, an academy, and a lot of werewolf porn. You can grab book 1 here.

Chaos, The Library of the Profane is available for pre-order now

The Library of the Profane has everything your black heart desires. But we don't just allow anyone to get a library card.

Need to summon a demon? Raise the dead? A clan of vampires bothering you? Do you like the really nasty werewolf erotica? The Library of the Profane has all of that, but not everyone can handle the contents (some people can't handle their werewolf erotica). I've been a librarian here for five years and when I say I killed to get this job, I'm not being facetious.

You can't check out our books. Some of the books are sentient and don't like it. We have rooms to perform the spells in, or hell, we do have a copy machine (copies are extra). When a witch came in and said they needed to do a little necromancy, I didn't question it. They wouldn't have been given a library card if they were going to raise someone really bad. I helped with the necromancy because it's just my job as a librarian.

Except it wasn't a normal resurrection. It was the physical embodiment of Chaos, and when he woke up, he saw me first and now he's attached. Chaos personified is a *horrible* library guest, and he won't leave with the witch who raised him. He's constantly getting into things he's not supposed to, and he's really into the werewolf erotica.

It's not like I can let him out because the Library of the Profane is meant to contain Chaos. The rest of the world isn't. He's awful about keeping his identity secret too. A warlock, a Hellhound, and a Vampire know he's here, and they are bugging me to let Chaos have a little fun.

I just want a normal day of summoning demons, cursing people, and telling people to be quiet in my library. This is too much.